HER SECOND CHANCE WOLF

OBSESSED MATES BOOK 5

ARIANA HAWKES

Imprint: Independently published

ISBN: 9798866370382

Cover art: Thunderface Design

www.arianahawkes.com

CONTENTS

Elinor

"Come see Umbilicus play at the Lowdown Bar!" I thrust a flyer at a guy with a long, yellowish beard and a biker gang vest.

"What?" He snatches it up and examines it, before shoving it back at me in disgust. "I'd rather tongue-kiss your grandma, Skinny Minnie."

"Heh, heh, heh," he cackles, swaggering into the venue.

Prick. I roll my eyes. I've been dealing with similar bullshit all night long. My boss has tasked me with dropping flyers outside what looks like an old school biker bar, while the band I'm promo-ing is pure emo. I tried to tell him, but he didn't listen, like always. And the best part is, these flyers contain discount codes, and if at least twenty percent of them don't get returned, then it's my fault and I'm out of a job.

This really sucks. I'm *good* at promo. I might even humbly say I'm the best promo chick in the county. For reasons:

Number one—I'm lightning-fast and scrappy as hell. *Shrug.* I'm a crow.

Two—I love music. Live gigs especially. The buzz, the energy. The tortured daydreams that I could be the one onstage instead.

And three—I'm ambitious. I need to make money right now. A ton of it. Which is why I can't just tell my boss to go screw himself.

Someone I care about a lot is sick, and I need to help pay for her to see specialists. Carolyn runs the kitchen at my main job—tending bar at *Sinner's Refuge*—and she and her sister Meredith are like family to me. A while back, Carolyn came down with some mysterious neurological disorder. Shifters don't often get sick, and no one can figure out what's wrong with her. We're real worried. Meredith keeps taking her to see different doctors around the country, and I figure the best thing I can do is earn as much money as I can.

So, here I am, trying to sell emo music to bikers.

The door of the venue swings open, and—whoa, what *is* that noise?

A ton of awful wailing and screeching guitars assaults my ears.

Yeeesh!

It's literally the worst band I've heard in my life. Are they tone deaf? It sounds like a banshee being tortured at the bottom of a well, while someone steps on a cat's tail—in slow motion.

Don't get me wrong, I love experimental music, unusual vocals, but this is just *bad*.

I give a shudder as the door closes again. Even I can sing better than that—

Well, I could if no one had to see me. If I could sing from backstage, or the restroom or something, while they put a pretty chick on the stage to lip-synch the vocals for me.

I snicker to myself. *Right, Elinor.* I'm sure there's plenty of call for that. Record companies will be falling over themselves to sign the weird-looking chick and her socially-acceptable stand-in—

And who on earth is in such a rush to get in there?

I watch as a guy hurtles out of the darkness, heading right at me. He's tall, dark, and he looks as mad as hell.

My bird fluffs up its feathers, going on high alert, but I force myself to stand my ground. He can't be mad at me. I'm not the one who's responsible for that terrible excuse for music.

When he gets close, I thrust out a flyer, repeat my spiel.

He seems like he's going to brush right past me, but at the last second, he snatches the flyer out of my hand. "Huh?" He frowns as he examines it, turning it every which way.

He's good-looking. Real good-looking, actually. All messy dark hair and angular features.

Then he gives me a long, intense look. Long enough to make me uncomfortable.

I know—I have weird, bulbous eyes. People stare at them a lot.

"Umbilicus? They sound like that?" He jerks his head toward the door.

"No, they're pretty cool, actually."

His frown deepens. "You promo this band?"

"Yeah."

"And who said you could be here?"

A drop of unease chases down my spine, but I plant my hands on my hips, push out my skinny bird chest, and make my voice strong and sassy. "It's standard. Everyone flyers at venues."

He grunts.

"You can check them out on YouTube."

"Maybe I will." His voice is a soft growl. And his gaze hasn't left me for a second.

Wolf shifter, I think. He has that lean, hungry look. And suddenly, I feel like a rabbit, caught in the sights of a predator.

There's something real familiar in his intense, light-colored eyes, though. Maybe I know him from Perdue—

"Nice jacket," he says.

"Whatever," I bite out. I'm used to people saying mean things about my clothes. It's a vintage leather biker jacket, and I've sewn a bunch of symbols and logos onto it. Yeah, it's quirky, but I love it.

His thick, black eyebrows shoot up. "I mean it."

"No, you don't."

His nostrils flare, like he's amused by me. "I do. I like your… your…" His gaze traces me from head to toe and back again. "Style," he finishes at last. "It's different. Catch you later."

Before I can open my mouth to reply, he's gone.

I stare at his retreating figure dazedly.

Catch you later.

What does that mean?

Kinda sounded like he was flirting. But guys who look like him don't flirt with girls who look like me.

I realize the awful noise has ended. The band must've finished their set.

So darn good when it stops.

A couple of guys in gang vests stroll along the pathway, and I hand the flyers to them, explain the discounts. They're kinda snarly at first, but eventually they take them, stuff them in their back pockets.

"Is the house band starting soon?" one of them asks.

I shrug. "I dunno. But someone just finished. Sounded like a cat being skinned alive."

He stares at me for a beat, then chokes out a laugh. "That's probably the warm-up act. The house band is better."

A few more guys arrive, some in leathers, others in lumberjack shirts. By the time the next band is getting ready to start, I've given out maybe a quarter of the flyers. Not great. It's gonna be a long night, and I'm on shift early tomorrow.

A big whoop goes up from inside the venue, followed by enthusiastic clapping and cheering.

A deep voice gives an intro, and another band roars to life. Not wailing this time, but actual music: rhythmic drums, thrashing guitars and powerful vocals.

Gooseflesh breaks out on my arms, as it always does when I hear something good. It's a cover song, but they're doing an awesome rendition.

I look around the lot. It's real quiet. There's no one to hand flyers to. Curiosity gets the better of me. I push open the doors and slip through.

The first song is finishing, and the room erupts into applause. And fuck—he's onstage:

The guy who just complimented my jacket. In low-slung black jeans, a leather jacket and a torn black T-shirt.

And my entire body jolts like I've been shocked—

Because now I know why he looked so familiar:

He's one of those assholes from high school who made my life a misery.

He looks different now—older, with longer hair—which is why I didn't recognize him right away, but he's one of *them*, no question.

I feel dizzy. There's not enough oxygen in the room. But somehow I've been walking toward him, pushing my way through the crowd, like I'm being propelled by an invisible force.

I stop, feet from the stage.

Blake Waldgrave.

His name drifts back like a malevolent spirit.

One of those jocks who used to hang around in their shifter gang, dominating sports, screwing cheerleaders and bullying the nerdy kids. Who never even noticed me until that day when I stood up to them, and all hell broke loose.

My cheeks burn hot as painful memories pour into

my mind, one after another. I hoped I'd never lay eyes on anyone from my high school days again. I even moved two states away to put the past behind me. But here it is again, like a slap in the face.

Can't believe I wondered whether he was flirting with me just now. Felt flattered even. An obnoxious dick who made my life hell.

I'm hot and panicky, and I need to get out of here before I pass out. I force my way back through the crowds, then I run outside and head for my car.

Screw the flyers, and the job.

I'll find some other way of making money.

I jog across the parking lot, stomach cramping with nausea.

But halfway there, I stop dead.

Elinor Earwood does not run away anymore!

I'm no longer that poor, nerdy kid—that baby bird abandoned in a cardboard box. So broken I'd never be able to shift properly. My animal's voice somehow stolen from my throat, so it can't communicate with me. I've been working on myself. I'm okay with who I am these days. I'm never gonna turn into a swan, but I've got a bunch of crow feathers protecting my heart, and people who depend on me.

Screw him.

No way am I going to let this prick chase me out of the job I need. No way am I going to let Carolyn down.

I turn another one-eighty and storm back to face him.

2

Elinor

"*H*ey—!"

Someone grabs my arm as I pass through the entrance again. A big, meaty security dude.

I spin, elbows out, aiming for his ribs. "Get the hell off of me!"

"Whoa." He throws up his hands. "Take it easy."

"What are you doing?" I snap.

"I've been told to look out for you. To keep you here."

"Like a prisoner?" My hand goes to my cellphone in my pocket. "Do I need to call the cops?"

"No, no. You're on the band's list, is all."

He shows me a clipboard with a list of names on it. At the bottom, someone has scrawled by hand: *Chick with edgy haircut and cool jacket.*

Literally those words. *WTF?*

"That you?" he says.

I blink. Then I fold my arms and nod slowly. Might as well own it. "Yeah, that's me."

"You can go backstage after the gig. Meet the band."

"Great," I say flatly.

Another song ends, and the applause is deafening.

Fuck.

The audience loves him.

Confident, charismatic. Holding them all in the palm of his big, werewolf hand.

Adult Blake Waldgrave is stupidly hot.

For a moment, I forget that I hate him, and I drink him in. The way the lights glance off the planes of his face. The way he shakes that black, tousled hair out of his eyes. The way those pale eyes blaze as they scan the audience.

And his voice... low and growly, vibrating all the way through me.

My heart is beating faster, and something weird is going on with my body. Bits of it are tingling and aching, in a way that's never happened before.

Fuck me dead.

He's an asshole, but an incredibly sexy asshole.

"This one's for the cool girl in the jacket," he growls.

And those eyes come to rest right on me.

I stop breathing altogether. He and his buddies made my life hell, and now he's serenading me? Confused doesn't begin to cut it.

But somehow I can't drag my own gaze away. I'm caught, like a rabbit in a trap, as the band plays the intro and he begins to sing. Lips close to the microphone, all his attention focused on me.

Oh god—and it's one of my old favorites, from my teenage years.

One of the songs I used to play when I was alone, consoling myself after a shitty day.

No, this can't be happening.

I should leave.

But I don't.

Instead, I stand there, and stare at Blake Waldgrave while he sings.

To me.

An inspirational song about how things will get better, and the future is full of sunshine and rainbows.

"No thanks to you, asshole," I mutter.

But still, my eyes keep running over him hungrily, zoning in on his crotch. I've always been a sucker for rock stars. That effortless sexiness, that attention-grabbing confidence. And he's got it in spades.

He's also gotten me aroused, goddamnit. I can tell my panties are a little wet.

I guess I came back because I wanted to see if it still hurt to look at him.

It does.

But hurt is not all I'm feeling, and I can't stand it.

I TEAR myself away and burst outside again. My cheeks are burning, and my body is all stirred up. The cold air is the slap in the face I needed. I hunch over and inhale big lungfuls of it.

Why the hell was he serenading me?

Is it some kind of joke at my expense?

It must be.

That's the only thing that makes any sense.

Some elaborate practical joke to entertain his friends. Some final act of revenge.

But what kind of freak gets turned on by shit like that?

Me, apparently.

The set continues. And I stand by the door, guts squirming, hearing the whole darn thing. Blake flirting with the audience. Owning the room. All the applause and adulation. The final song ending, the band leaving the stage. The rhythmic clapping and screams for "more!"

The encore goes on for three more songs. Pounding drums, thrashing guitars. And at long last, it's over. "Goodnight, guys. You've all been awesome," I hear Blake yell, and a few minutes later, people start to spill through the doors.

They're pumped from the gig, chattering about how good it was; girls gossiping about how *hot* the lead singer is.

It's easier to get people's attention now they're excitable and drunk, and I force myself to go super-fast, shoving the flyers in their faces and explaining the discounts at a hundred miles an hour.

And… I'm done.

I've given my last flyer away while people are still wandering out of the venue.

Good job, girl, I tell myself. Now I can get the hell out

of here.

But, as I ease through a bunch of people chatting, smoking and discussing where to go drinking next, a couple of voices rise up above the others.

"Ronny, I don't want to do this. Blake's a nice guy—" This is coming from a blonde cheerleader-type in a skin-tight dress.

Blake?

I slide into the shadows and listen.

"I don't give a damn. You wanna make this happen, or am I just wasting my time on you?" replies an older dude with a lean, pockmarked face.

Blonde chick sighs and rolls her eyes. "Okay. Tell me what I need to do."

He leans closer to her. "When Blake comes out, you go up to him, tell him you've been cheating on him with his best friend—who's that guy?"

"Ed," she supplies.

"Yeah. You tell him you've been screwing Ed. Riding his nice big dick. He freaks out, grabs you or some shit. I snap a few pics. Send 'em to my contacts. You wake up tomorrow, and your Insta feed is blowing up. *Instant fame.*"

She grimaces and chews on her lip. "But, what if he doesn't freak out? What if he doesn't give a shit?"

His eyes narrow. "He's a were, right?"

"Yeah."

"He'll freak out, trust me. They're possessive fuckers."

She exhales loudly. "I dunno. Seems like Blake's not that *into* me."

The guy leans back and scans her up and down. "Gotta work your assets, honey. That's what god made 'em for."

She grins stupidly, lit up by his cheap compliment.

Shit.

She's going to set up Blake, to advance her own trashy career?

And wow, why do I even care?

I'm still finishing that thought when a door at the side of the building opens, and Blake emerges. My gut tightens. Silently, I watch as he scans the crowd.

"Blake, over here!" the girl hollers, arms thrown wide.

Blake's gaze flicks to her, and away again. He's looking for something—

Me.

The realization comes with a lurch.

I'm not easy to spot where I'm standing, but that pale gaze locks onto mine, and I shudder. I freaking shudder. He strides toward me and I'm frozen. Rooted to the spot.

"Blake, I'm *here*!" Desperation tinges the girl's voice as she darts in front of him, flashing a huge smile, all shiny teeth and pumped-up lips.

Annoyance flickers in his handsome features as he stops and takes her in. "What's up Paige?"

She turns her head, looking for her cameraman, then she flings her arms around his neck. "I wanted to tell you something!"

Rage courses through me. Blake might be an asshole,

but if there's one thing I hate as much as bullying, it's lying and cheating.

"Whatever she tells you, she's full of shit," I say. "She and her promo guy just planned the whole thing."

Blake goes still, then his eyes dart to me again. "What?"

I push up off the wall and come toward him. "She wants to make you mad, so you'll hit her or something."

His nostrils flare and his jaw juts out.

"She's planning on telling you she's been screwing your best friend," I continue.

He unleashes a roar of fury. And he charges.

A second later, an expensive camera is smashing on the ground. Blake shoves the cameraman, knocking him off his feet. Then he rounds on the cheerleader.

Her eyes are glittering with a mixture of fear and excitement, but they dart around the crowd, before settling on him again. She's hoping someone else is filming the scene, of course. "That's right, Blake. I was just using you for my own career. Doesn't that make you mad?"

Blake snorts. "Your *career*? Paige, you don't have a career. There's not a scrap of talent in that pretty little head of yours." He curls his lip. "And Ed's gay, you nitwit."

He turns his back on her.

Then he walks right over to me.

My mouth is hanging open, but I snap it shut as he approaches.

"Thank you," he says.

"You're welcome." I shrug nonchalantly, like my

heart isn't pounding all the way up in my throat. "Com-miserations on your breakup."

He makes a dismissive sound. "We weren't *together*."

"She seemed to think you were."

His lip curls again and he shakes his head dismis-sively. "Wish I could say I'm surprised at that shit she just pulled."

"Guess their bet didn't pay off."

"What bet?"

"They bet you were as possessive as hell."

He gives a low, throaty growl. "Oh, I am possessive." His eyes burn into mine. "No one touches what's mine."

I swallow hard and gooseflesh breaks out on my skin. If I didn't know better, I'd think he was talking about me.

But that's ridiculous.

I drag my gaze away from him, remembering that I hate his guts.

"Anyway, I wasn't trying to help you. I just hate lying and cheating, is all. Good deed done. So long." I force myself into a one-eighty, and I flounce off toward my car.

"Wait." A huge hand encircles my upper arm. A huge, callused hand. I swear I can feel the heat coming through my jacket.

"Why?" I snap.

His lips part but no sound comes out. He looks taken aback. *Ha.* I bet Blake Waldgrave has never been taken aback in his life before.

"You can't leave."

I tear my arm away. "What are you talking about?"

His lips work. No way am I noticing how stupidly lush they are. "I need your help."

Help?

"What do you mean?"

"With—" He breaks off, his nostrils flaring. "With promo," he says quickly.

Oh. And now I'm extra mad at myself.

My body sags. Because there was that dumb, dumb part of me that thought he might be attracted to me. But he wants me to hand out flyers for him or something.

Of course he's not interested in you, weirdo.

"Get someone else," I say.

His pupils dilate as they take me in. "No. You... you're not like everyone else."

"Yeah, I've been hearing that all my life—"

Those words start churning through my brain again: *Weirdo. Freak. Loser.*

"—And, guess what, I'm done hearing it!"

My voice is shrill. My crow's caw. And it knocks him backward. But I don't care.

"Leave me alone, Blake Waldgrave!"

My heart twists and my feathers begin to unfurl. I sprint for my car before I have one of my awful, ugly, broken-bird shifts.

3

Blake

I can't eat. I can't sleep.

It's been three days since I first laid eyes on my little birdie, and she's all I can think about. That glossy, jet-black hair, those big, wide-set eyes. All those cool, quirky tattoos and piercings.

I'm a sick man. I don't even know her name, but those bright black eyes of hers fill every thought. She's nothing like any chick I've met before, and I'm totally fixated on her.

The moment I saw her standing outside JC's, my wolf's mating urge roared to life for the first time.

And when she walked inside and our eyes locked, I was lost.

She's so tiny, vulnerable. I feel like I could lift her up and put her on my shoulder. But so full of fire and sass. I never pictured myself with a bird. Not sure if I ever truly pictured myself with anyone. All my encounters with women have been so hollow. Paige was just the latest in a long line of chicks who wanted to be with me because it brought them kudos, or something. They all wanted to be seen with me, screwed by me.

And this little bird acted like she didn't give a shit.

And she was so edgy and hostile, I would've believed her.

If I hadn't seen her watching me on stage. She focused on my every move, with a bird's intensity. Her eyes didn't stray from me once.

I took in her parted lips; her small hand, rising to her chest, as if she was measuring the speed of her heartbeat.

She was too far away for me to smell her scent, but I picked it up later—sweet and heady, and I knew: she wanted me.

Every song I sang was just for her. The crowd thought I was running through the usual favorites. But I picked a song that means a lot to me. I was calling her to me.

I put her on my guestlist, hoping she'd join me backstage.

But she didn't come, because she's sassy like that.

Then she protected me. And the weird thing is, I didn't care that I was the object of some dumb manipulation. All I could think was how awesome my girl is. How fearless and outspoken.

My mate.

My beast has never spoken the word before, but now it won't quit insisting.

Find her.

Get to her.

It's ready to take matters into its own hands. Threatening to burst out of me and hunt her down. It's all I can do to keep it inside me.

I've been asking around, but no one knows her name. No one's ever seen her before. She's not an MC chick, that's for sure.

All I have of hers is the band flyer she gave me. I've memorized every single word of it. Pressed it to my nose, inhaling the faintest traces of her scent. The band is playing in a couple of days, but I can't wait that long to try and find her. Some other dude might have snatched her away by then.

My knuckles crunch at the thought.

For three days, I've been looking for her from dawn till midnight. I've been driving around every small town in a radius around JC's, asking if anyone knows her. I also have a single, crappy photo. After she ran out on me, I sat down in the office and trawled through the CCTV, trying to get a good image of her. The system is old, though—we inherited it along with the club—and the only shot where you can see her face is black and white and grainy as hell.

My dad is mad at me. This is no time to be abandoning my work. For a long time, I've been struggling to turn his seedy old MC bar into a real music venue. We're just starting to see results, but we're still barely breaking even.

But I don't give a crap. Nothing is worth having without my mate.

I know if I don't find this girl, I'll lose my drive. I won't be able to help out by singing in the house band. And I'll go back to that dark, dark place I fell into after high school.

IT'S ALREADY DARK when a turn-off for Perdue catches my eye. I've heard it's a place for unique personalities. People who don't want to follow society's rules. Seems like the kind of place my little bird might have her roost.

I flick my blinker and take the exit off the highway.

It's a small town of a few thousand, I guess, made up of narrow, mazelike streets. Like it's doing its best to confuse outsiders.

My wolf's ears are pricked up, nose twitching.

I'm on the right track. I feel it deep in my chest. A low vibrating growl. My beast calling to its mate.

I trawl the streets, looking for bars, gathering places. Does she work in an office during the day? I picture her sitting at a desk, tapping away at a computer. I'll bet she's real good at her job. Whip smart and efficient.

A lot of the stores are dark, with shutters pulled down, or bars at the windows. A tattoo shop still has its lights on. When I pull up, a big, unfriendly-looking guy hauls open the door and glowers at me.

"Is there a promo company in town? Or a marketing agency?" I call through the window of my truck.

"Who wants to know?" His gaze fixates on my out-of-state plates.

"I'm looking for a small chick, black hair. Chopped right here." I try to indicate my girl's sharp hairstyle, and I thrust out the sheet of paper with her image on it.

The guy snarls, strides right over, and snatches the paper out of my hand.

My wolf's hackles rise as it scents another Alpha wolf. *Easy,* I tell it.

His hostile face fills the window. "*Friendly* word of advice. Don't go asking about people in this town. If you know what's good for you, you'll turn around and go back the way you came."

My wolf snarls. I cage it behind my teeth, but it's too late. It bursts from my lips with a feral sound.

The guy's own beast rises, the bones in his face broadening. "Don't make me fight you, stranger. I'm the unofficial law around here, and it won't end well."

My wolf claws up my insides, its fur burning my skin. I push back on it. "I don't want to fight anyone. I'm just looking for my mate."

His eyebrows lift. "Your mate?" He looks at the photo for a long, long time. "Can't help," he says at last.

My beast growls. He's lying.

His eyes lock onto mine. "Some folks here have suffered a lot," he says slowly. "It's my job to make sure no one hurts them anymore. You wanna get in touch with her, use the Internet or some shit like that."

Before I can reply, he turns and stomps back to his tattoo shop, slamming the door behind him.

She's here.

People are protecting her.

That gives me some comfort—

My job to protect her! my wolf bellows. I shove it back down, but it's right.

All the tattoo shop dude's warning has done is make me more determined to find her.

Anticipation runs like lava in my veins. She's here. In this town. All I have to do is track her down.

I'm not giving up.

I'M MORE CAUTIOUS NOW, though. I know better than to flash her photo around. Instead, I just look.

A night passes. I sleep in my car, on the outskirts of the town. All day, I lay low, avoiding attracting attention to myself. I wander around streets like a tourist. It's a weird town. Most of it is dark, shuttered, hostile. But there are a bunch of new shops and a little bookstore that looks like it's been teleported from some cute college town. I hope my girl's been happy living here. I hope no one's been trying to steal her heart.

When it gets dark, I go hunt again.

At last, I strike gold. A little bar on a narrow backstreet. Sinner's Refuge.

There she is.

Working behind the bar, pouring beers.

My breath catches at the sight of her. Warmth floods my chest.

I've thought about her so long and hard; I can hardly believe I'm seeing her with my own eyes.

Her hair hangs loose to her shoulders, dead straight,

and she's wearing a black pinafore dress over a stripy black-and-white sweater. She's so individual, my girl. She likes doing everything her own way.

I hang in the shadows and watch her through a window.

She's quick, full of energy. When she's done putting the drinks on a tray, she dashes them over to a table. Then she's back, serving some guys at the bar.

My beast growls. There are a lot of guys in there. Hungry, feral shifters. It doesn't like that, one bit.

But it likes watching *her*.

My mate.

Hectic and full of life, black, glossy hair swinging like a curtain as she moves. And she's good with the customers. She's less than half the size of most of the beasts in there, but she doesn't take shit from anyone. Her mouth is sassy and her elbows are sharp. I'm entranced by every single thing she does.

Never thought my mate would be a bird, but now it just seems *right*.

I start to imagine our life together. I'll take her back to my hometown, renovate my big old family house for her. We'll have a whole litter of pups. Half-wolf, half-bird. That'll be a cool combination. They'll all have her jet-black hair and big eyes.

Every nerve in my body yearns to storm in there and tell her she's mine. Sweep her out in my arms. But I've got to be patient. She's flighty and I don't want to scare her off again.

There's a sound behind me—a quiet tread.

I whirl around.

Crack!

Too late. Something socks me in the side of the head.

I roar in pain and fury, and I find myself staring right into the fierce brown eyes of a big mama-bear shifter. *She cuffed me?*

My beast is pushing its way out, canines breaking through, fur burning my skin, but I rein it back in. "What the fuck?" I bellow instead.

She doesn't falter one bit. "Why have you been stalking that girl?" she demands, looking like she's about to rip my head off.

"What girl—?"

"Don't play dumb." Her expression is shrewd. "Unless you want things to get real messy."

She knows her. She's protective of her. They're not blood relations, obviously. But maybe she's her guardian or something. My mind whirls. Don't want to end up on the wrong side of my girl's adoptive mother.

"She's my mate," I say at last.

The bear's eyebrows shoot up. "Your *mate?*" There's a mocking tone in her voice that my wolf does not appreciate. It's fine. I can deal. I can deal with anything for the sake of my girl.

"And that's why you've been staring at her through the window like a pervert?"

"I'm keeping watch over her," I snarl.

She shakes her head slowly. ""That's *my* job, wolf features. Elinor has people to keep watch over her."

Elinor.

That's my angel's name. It fizzes and sparkles in my heart like a firework show.

I repeat it in my head over and over, while darts of longing set me alight.

"She doesn't know she's your mate, does she?" the mama bear cuts in. Her voice is dripping with sarcasm.

The old me would've ripped into her. But I hold back.

"I've come to claim her."

She looks me up and down, nostrils flaring while her massive lungs inflate. "A lot of guys think Elinor is their mate. They've all been wrong. And most of them have ended up barred from here. From the whole town, in fact."

My wolf roars at the thought of other men trying to claim her.

Play nice, I remind it.

"I'm different."

She looks me up and down again. "You don't look like her type."

"What do you—?"

"You look like an overgrown frat boy. The kind of guy who'll break her heart."

"Never!" I roar. "She's mine."

She takes a step closer, until I can see the flecks of gold in her irises. "I don't know about you. You're not the kind of guy I imagined her with. I don't know if you're right for her."

"Trust me, I'm going to make her happy."

She curls her lip. "You want to claim a girl like her, you work for it. And you screw up, you've got me to deal with. Now, don't let me see you creeping around here again."

Before I can reply, she turns on her heel and leaves.

My wolf is all growly and snarly. Offended she could think I'm not the perfect mate for my girl. I take one last, lingering glance through the window. There she is —Elinor—chatting to some chick across the bar counter. Her face all lit up, and she's giggling, like they're sharing some gossip.

A deep ache blooms in my chest. *Mate.*

I swear I'm going to make her the happiest woman alive.

And then I'll make her mine.

4

Elinor

I feel twitchy. I mean, I always feel twitchy. I'm a bird. Hyper-alertness is in my DNA. But today I feel *extra* twitchy. More like agitated and uneasy.

"Watch out for smooth-talking strangers," Meredith told me as she left to take Carolyn to yet another doctor's appointment. That was right after she gave me a massive hug and thanked me for everything I'm doing. She doesn't need to thank me. She's basically my mom, and I owe her my whole life. And Carolyn is kind of like my auntie, and I'm real worried about her. Whenever I tell myself I'm too tired to go do promo after my shifts at Sinner's, I remember that we've got to do everything we can to help her get better.

One good thing that's happened is I have a new

roommate. Tiana is a sweet girl, and turns out she used to be a short-order chef. So, she's working in the kitchen now, which is great. Before she started, we had to shut the kitchen down some days because it was impossible for me to cook the food and run the bar by myself.

So, it's actually pretty quiet in here for once. I try to keep busy, polishing all the glasses and the silverware, but my birdy-senses are tingling and my attention keeps flitting around the room.

Of course, my bird hasn't been able to settle since three nights ago, when Blake Waldgrave crashed back into my life. All those memories I thought I'd stuffed in a deep, dark place burst out again, and my mind has not been a peaceful place. At all.

I wasn't always a target for bullies at high school. Yeah, I had scraggy braids and thick glasses, and I might've walked out of the school bathroom with my skirt tucked into my pantyhose one time. But mostly, I was just a quiet kid who grew up in foster care.

I got rejected by my birth family. I was thrown out of the family nest—literally. Someone found me in a cardboard box on the sidewalk and took me to a fire station. One of my foster parents' real kids told me this one day, full of glee. *You were so ugly, no one wanted you. All scrawny, with those big, weird bird eyes*. She found the social worker's report in my foster parents' files and showed it to me. It was all true.

The cardboard box contained a note saying, *Not one of ours. Darn cuckoo must've laid an egg in our nest.*

I was lucky someone handed me over to the authorities, and I didn't just get thrown in the trash.

None of the foster families wanted to keep me. I was too weird looking. Too introverted. I kept running away and trying to get back to the family that didn't want me. I don't remember this part so well, but apparently I kept getting obsessed with people I thought were my family, and trying to break into their houses.

Eventually, I got sent to a group home and I spent the last six years of my childhood there. It wasn't so bad. People pretty much ignored me. And at high school, it was the same. I was just a weird loser. Then as I got older, I realized I was smart. I was good at math and English.

And that turned out to be my downfall.

After that, things got real bad. Bags of shit dumped in my locker. Porn pictures stuffed in my schoolbag. Kids spitting on my lunch tray. High school was like one giant booby trap. Everywhere I went, there were feet stuck out to trip me; braying laughter in my wake—

Creak—

The bar's front door opens. Darn hinges need oiling.

I turn around to greet our latest customer—

And freeze.

It's him:

Standing in the doorway. Sexy as hell in a fresh white T-shirt that shows off his massive shoulders and chest. His glowing, pale eyes lock onto mine, and all I can do is stare.

My brain has turned to mush. Guess it's still

processing the fact that the guy I've been fretting about all morning in now right here in front of him.

He looks so good, I want to punch him.

A half-smile tugs at one corner of his ridiculously lush lips, and he strolls up to the counter.

I back up a bunch of steps and scowl at him.

"What are you doing here?" I demand, trying to ignore the tremors that have taken hold of me. My body is lighting up in his presence. I know it means something, and I don't appreciate it one bit.

"Looking for you," he says simply, and his gaze traces across my features. Somehow it feels like a caress, and I can't stand it. I'm disgusted with myself.

"I thought I told you to leave me alone!" I spit out.

He narrows his eyes. Which makes him look even sexier. "I believe your exact words were, leave me alone, Blake Waldgrave."

A dart of alarm goes through me. I'd forgotten that part.

My crow ruffles her feathers, tries to look intimidating. "That's your name."

"But how did *you* know that?"

I work my jaw back and forth. He has absolutely no idea who I am. And that just makes me as mad as hell.

I wasn't planning to tell him, but the words tumble out:

"We were at high school together."

He stiffens, his pupils constricting. I watch his face, waiting for that spark of recognition to appear, followed by the inevitable disgust.

But his face remains blank. His confusion is almost cute.

Almost.

He tilts his head, kind of playfully. "Are you sure—?"

"How did you find me here?"

A ghost of a grin chases across those lush lips of his. "I asked around pretty much all the towns between here and Arndale. This was the only one where people told me to fuck off. Figured I had to be on the right track."

I stare at him in confusion. He seems so cool. Self-deprecating. Nothing like that arrogant asshole I remember from high school.

His smile gets broader.

That winning smile that gave all the girls wet panties. Well, not me.

"I came to tell you, I mean *good* different. And I'm sorry if I offended you."

"You don't remember me at all, do you?" I come up to the bar. "Which is kind of funny, because I still think about you and your friends real often."

I brace my hands on the bartop. My heart is beating so hard it's making me dizzy.

"Let's rewind to…oh, seven years ago." I give a mock dreamy sigh.

"I and all my nerdy friends were busting our asses at high school. Finishing our assignments on time. Trying to get good grades. Meanwhile, a bunch of jocks were fucking around, playing sports, failing at school. Losing out on college scholarships.

"And one day, one of these jocks came up with an amazing idea: why not get the smart kids to do our work for us? So they hired a bunch of us to do their homework for them. To write their papers, take tests. I use the term *hired* loosely, because the poor kids didn't get any choice in the matter. They got bullied, threatened. Forced to work long hours. Some of them were only sleeping three hours a night.

"I could take it. I'm a tough bird. But some of my friends weren't. They were getting real run down. Their grades started to slip, because they didn't get enough time to do their own work. And I hated to see my friends like that. So, I bust the whole essay-writing ring wide open—"

Blake is staring at me so hard, the hairs on the back of my neck are prickling, but I'm not going to quit now.

"I had a confidential conversation with the principal, explaining what was going on. And it worked. The nerdy kids got their lives and college dreams back. But someone found out that I was the whistleblower, and my life turned to shit."

His massive chest swells, and I see his animal surfacing. This might be the final moment of my life, before he tears me apart. Every nerve in my body tells me to run, but I stay stock still, fix my glare on his light irises.

"You were that skinny little chick with long braids," he says at last. "You always used to wear those plaid skirts."

I nod slowly. "Yup."

"That was you," he breathes, and he scans me over and over, as if he's trying to square the two versions of me.

I squirm under his scrutiny, and I hold my breath

because, despite everything, a stupid part of me can't stand to see disgust flickering across his face.

"I'll be damned," he mutters, half to himself. "The girl who felled the whole football team."

"Elinor?" Tiana, the chef, calls from the kitchen. "Can you help?"

"What is it?" I go to see what she needs.

When I return, the front door is swinging wide open, and he's gone.

Now he remembers me, he can't stand the sight of me.

"Good riddance," I mutter. But when I grab a glass from the dishwasher, it slips out of my hand and shatters on the ground.

5

Blake

Twenty-five beer kegs down; another twenty-five to go. It's a crisp fall morning, but sweat is pouring into my eyes and running down my back. I pause to wipe my face with my T-shirt. The whole darn thing is drenched. I rip it off and stuff it into the back of my pants. Instantly, I feel better. If I had my way, I wouldn't wear clothes at all. A whole life spent in civilization, and my beast is still as wild as any dominant were. And right, now it snatches up any outlet for freedom.

Ever since I found out who Elinor really is, it's been unbearable. It keeps insisting that she's its mate—of course. It doesn't understand how everything changed the moment she leaned across the bartop and spoke those words.

It seems incredible, but I didn't recognize her at all. And to be honest, I still can't square this beautiful feisty chick with the malnourished little kid in braids and glasses from high school.

But when my girl's eyes filled with such pain, and hatred *for me*, my chest seized up; I couldn't breathe. I thought my bones would crumble. My beast was fighting its way out, and I had to get out of there.

I've found my mate, and she hates my guts.

Because of what I did.

"Come on, kid. We've gotta be done in the next hour."

I direct a snarl at my dad. I'm trying my damnedest to be patient with him, but my nerves are already frayed, and he seems to know exactly how to pluck at them.

"You're lucky I'm helping you at all," I growl, grabbing another keg from the back of the truck.

He snarls right back at me and snatches up the keg next to mine. Almost seventy, and his wiry strength is as relentless as ever. "Some help," he mutters, half under his breath.

"What!?" I roar. I drop the keg I'm carrying and straighten up, my beast itching to come out and challenge him.

He's too much. Ever since he bought this notorious biker bar, with his crazy plan to transform it into a 'modern' music venue, I've been stuck here, helping him.

He turns to face me, and I see his own beast pushing

up beneath his lean, angular features. "You really screwed up the other day."

"Huh?" I literally have no idea what he's talking about.

"That publicity stunt I set up."

I stare at him for several beats. "*You* set up that dumb stunt with Paige?" I stare at my grizzled father in disbelief, rage pouring through me like molten lava.

"Coulda blown up on Insta. If it wasn't for you."

I shake my head violently. "On what?"

"Instagram, son. All the kids are into it nowadays." He shakes his own head. "It's all about making an impact."

I unleash a wild roar and charge at him. "Not. That. Kind. Of Impact. You want to market this as a place where the owner's son abuses women?"

He goes still, and I can almost see the cogs of his brain turning. "Paige was down with it."

I snarl through my teeth. "I'm sorry to say that chick is down with anything that means she get attention." I unleash a groan of desperation. "That's not how things work nowadays."

"The promo guy told me there's a few fighting celebs out there. Never did their careers any harm. Helped 'em take off, in fact."

I slap my hand against my forehead. "Dad, we are not the Kardashians. We're trying to build a reputable music business here. This is the wrong type of publicity—"

I break off. I'm clenching my fists so tight, they hurt. I feel like punching a wall.

I'm okay with the fact that this place is my business now. The fact is, I needed something. I crashed hard after everything that happened at high school. Unlike my buddies, I could've still gone to a good college—I started working hard and I got the grades. But I didn't go. I lost my place in the world, and I ended up drifting for a few years. My dad was so disappointed in me. He'd grown up a lone wolf, kicked out of his own pack for some political bullshit I've never understood, and we were vulnerable, unprotected. He was so proud of me for being the first one in our bloodline to have college aspirations. And I think he's never forgiven me for throwing it all away. Which is why I've got to make a success of this darn bar.

My dad's idea to invest his life savings in an entertainment venue was a good one. I just wished he'd consulted me before he decided to purchase a notorious biker bar, with a ready-made clientele, who aren't taking kindly to the news that the place is under new management.

We've had to deal with a lot of shit since we've opened. A biker gang threatening to burn the place down if we don't turn it back to 'how it used to be'. AKA, the stinking pile of crap that they unofficially made their clubhouse. Complete with a rancid cellar spattered with bloodstains. I can't even—

"You could be big, kid. You should see the way everyone watches you when you're up on stage."

I groan. We've had this conversation at least ten times before. "I'm not a rockstar, dad. I'm just helping out until you hire a house band."

"Won't be as good as you."

"Dad, I don't even write my own songs." I give a dismissive grunt and yank the keg off the ground again. I guess I've got an okay voice, and I enjoy singing other people's stuff, but that's all. I've ever been good at composing shit. Never wanted to.

"You could get someone to help—"

"Enough!" I roar.

I'm full to the brim with his crazy ideas. If I hear one more, I might explode.

"What's the matter with you? Why you so wound up?" Dad comes up behind me.

"I'm not," I snap.

But he's right.

I am.

Of course, I am.

I was lucky enough to have met my mate at high school. And instead of claiming her, I bullied her and made her life a misery.

We were such assholes.

I was young and dumb, and that's no excuse at all.

Back in those days, my shifter buddies and I were kings of the school, and we knew it. All the other kids worshipped us. The guys wanted to be us; the girls wanted to screw us. And, being the dumb teenagers we were, we let it go to our heads. Our football team was unbeatable. We totally crushed all the other schools in the state. All of us had college sports scholarships waiting for us.

And all of us were failing at school. We were too busy reveling in all the adulation. Training, going to parties, dating girls. School was just a pain in our asses, because we all knew that we weren't planning to work with our brains. We were gonna be college football stars, then national champions.

Then my buddy Jeff, hit on the great idea of getting the other kids to do our work for us.

It was a great solution—at least at first. We paid them. Well, Jeff did because his parents were loaded. The school was in a deprived area, and a lot of those poor nerdy kids needed the money. My brain was small, my conscience was clear. And call me dumb, because I really was, but I had no idea that some of the kids were being bullied into working more than they wanted to.

Then everything fell apart. One brave kid blew the whistle on all the cheating, and for a bunch of us, our football dreams were over. Jeff—identified as the ring-leader—was kicked out of school. Most of the other guys were allowed to stay, but they kept failing and they lost their college places.

And of course, they were mad as hell—not at them-selves, though. Instead, they took it out on Elinor.

I wasn't one of the kids who did bad stuff to her. But I didn't do anything to stop them. And I know that makes me as guilty as they are. That's the burden I have to carry.

I'd do anything to take it all back.

To remove the pain from her eyes.

But how can I do that when I'm the one who put it there?

I don't deserve Elinor.

She's mine. I feel it with every nerve in my body. But

that hatred on her face, when she told me how she knew me, cut me to the quick.

I've lost the right to call her my mate.

I'll never be able to claim her.

I can't stay away from her, though.

Every day, I drive back to Perdue Town. Hide in the shadows, watching her working in the bar, or going home to her apartment, or meeting up with her friends. I'm so in awe of what she's made of herself. Of the cool, sassy chick she's blossomed into.

I should quit doing this.

All I'm doing is making my animal worse. Firing its longing for her.

But maybe this is what I deserve—eternal torment.

I vow I'll protect her forever, even if I can't make her mine.

6

Elinor

He's here.
I'm sure of it.

A whisper of his spicy, exciting scent drifts past my nostrils.

I spin around, heart pounding as my gaze flits around the darkened venue.

I can't see him.

No one is as tall, as broad-shouldered.

As ridiculously sexy.

For days I've been getting this feeling that Blake is watching me. At work, around Perdue. But when I turn around, he's never there.

Maybe I'm paranoid. Worried he's going to try and take revenge on me or something.

I'm working at the Umbilicus gig, and the band has

been keeping me busy all evening. Treating me like I'm their personal assistant or something. Sending me to the bar to order them a gazillion rounds of JD and coke. Getting me to pass on all kinds of special requests.

I mean, I'm not complaining. All work is good work. But it's not really what their manager hired me to do.

And every moment, I'm in danger of monumentally screwing up, because I can't quit thinking about my bully and what he's doing here.

Is he stalking me? Trying to intimidate me?

Is he even here at all? Ever since he crashed back into my life, my head has been in a real weird place. I won't be so surprised if I've started hallucinating.

"Hey, girlie—!"

I don't acknowledge the lead singer's loud, insolent voice. I've told him my name a bunch of times.

"Hey!" Even louder. "I'm talking to you, goddamnit!"

My bird's feathers ruffle, and I finally flip around before something ugly happens.

I plant my hands on my hips. "Excuse me, *Elinor.*" My voice drips with sarcasm.

"Yeah—" He holds out his empty glass, shaking the ice cubes so they clink around like a bell. "Told you to keep our glasses topped up."

I clench my teeth. He's already drunk. They all are. And before they go on stage, they'll probably snort another bunch of coke to wake themselves up. This was not what I signed up for. At all.

But... money. I force myself to think of Carolyn. Of the appointment she had earlier today. We were real hopeful that the specialist would be able to help her, but, like all the others, he couldn't find anything wrong.

"Another round of JDs coming right up," I mutter between my teeth, and I snatch up the glass, resisting the urge to toss the ice cubes in his face.

Umbilicus are a bunch of fucking entitled pricks.

I've already had to ignore the lines of coke racked up on the coffee table, and the fact that one of them was literally screwing a groupie in the corner of the room.

I push my way through the crowd to get to the bar.

A warm-up act is playing and the place is heaving, mainly with kids too young to buy alcohol.

I yell my order across the bar, tell the bartender they're free drinks for the band.

He raises an eyebrow, since it's at least the tenth round tonight, but loads up a tray for me.

I carry it back, dodging flying elbows. Thank goodness I've had plenty of practice dealing with the rowdy shifters at Sinner's.

Off to my left, three teenage boys are jumping in time to the music. Arms around each other's shoulders… boing… boing… boing…like a big, clumsy missile. They're getting closer and closer to me. Far too goddamn close.

"Watch out!" I yell, but my voice disappears beneath the music. I try to scuttle out of the way, but the place is rammed. There's nowhere to go. *Boing!* Another jump brings them right in my path. I turn my back on them to protect the full tray of drinks, at the exact moment that all three of them crash into me.

"Argh!" I yell, as the impact knocks me off my feet.

Smash! go ten quadruple JDs and cokes, a split second before I land right on top of them.

Fuck.

Just then, the lead singer's head pokes through the door that leads to the backstage area.

He takes me in, lip curling. "Where the fuck have you been?" he bellows.

I stare back at him, stunned. I'm sitting in a pool of fizzy liquid, and my ass is prickling from the broken glass.

"Are you freaking kidding me—?" I yell back, but the end of my sentence is drowned out by a feral roar.

It's coming from behind me.

My bird heart pounds in my chest: It's him.

No question, no uncertainty this time.

I twist my head around.

Blake Waldgrave is standing right there, behind me. His massive arms are holding two of the teenagers by the scruffs of their necks. Their feet are barely touching the ground. Guess *that's* why they didn't land right on top of me, I think dazedly.

"What the hell were you thinking?" he roars. "You want to jump around like that, you go to a mosh pit." He shakes them hard. "Look what you've done to her."

Three sets of eyes stare at me, wide with terror.

"I'm sorry," one of them says.

"Yeah, I'm real sorry. I wasn't thinking."

"Be more careful," Blake tells them. "Not everyone's as big and dumb as you are. Especially women."

They nod fearfully, and he dumps them in a heap,

like discarded garbage. Then he comes to me, hands outstretched. "Elinor, come here."

Despite the fact I'm sitting in a sticky, spiky puddle, I'm not planning on accepting his help.

But, suddenly, one arm is curling around my back, the other is tucked behind my knees, and he's sweeping me up.

He doesn't set me on my feet right away, but continues to hold me, gazing deep into my eyes. His breathing is ragged, like he's been running, and his scent fills my nostrils. It shouldn't feel this good to be close to him.

My heart is pounding so hard I might pass out. I'm helpless in his arms. Hypnotized by the magnetic power of his animal.

Mate.

What?

The word appears in my brain, fully formed, and my whole body spasms. Did my bird say that? It never speaks—to me or anyone else.

"I'm good," I tell him. "You can put me down."

"Are you sure?" His voice is tender, and it sends a thrill right through me.

"Yeah. Nothing a change of clothes won't fix." I give a dry laugh.

He gently deposits me back on the ground. "Are you hurt?" he tries to turn me around, check the back of my pants.

"Stop—" I pull away with an embarrassed laugh.

"Get me another round!" a loud, stupid voice slurs.

Both our heads snap toward the leader singer, who's still lounging in the doorway.

"Are you kidding me?" Blake roars.

The guy blinks. "Who the fuck do you think you're talking to?"

Blake moves so fast, he's a blur of denim and leather and black hair. One second he's standing right beside me, the next he's pinning the leader singer against the door frame by his throat.

"Don't you dare speak to Elinor like that, you piece of crap," he growls. "You think she's here to wait on you? You think that's why she was hired?"

The singer's bloodshot eyes bulge and he grunts something. Blake releases his grip on his throat. "What?"

He grabs at his throat. "She's the promo chick," he wheezes.

"Exactly. She's here to help you sell more albums, not to run around all night bringing you drinks. You ever speak to her like that again, I'll rip your throat out. Literally. You hear me?"

The singer nods vigorously.

"She's not working for you anymore, so you can give her a nice severance package."

"I need her, though," the singer stutters. He turns his head, looking for me. "Elinor, I'm sorry, okay. I'll get my manager to give you a pay rise or something."

Blake roars. "Get the hell out of my sight!"

He doesn't need telling twice. He dashes into the backroom, slamming the door behind him.

"What the fuck?" I shout, my voice all shrill and bird-like.

Blake turns back to me, eyes still full of fire.

I plant my hands on my hips. "Thank you for scraping me off the floor and all. But you have no right to quit my job for me."

He shakes his head. "You're not working for him anymore."

"You don't get to decide that—"

"You're working for me."

What?"

"*I* need you, Elinor." His voice is throaty, raw, and suddenly he drops, and he's on his knees in front of me, amid all the glass and spilled drinks. He's so tall that we're about on eye level. My heart thumps at his closeness. At the way his lush lips are inches from mine.

My breath catches in my throat. I should not be feeling like this.

I shake my head to get rid of these thoughts. "Have you forgotten what I told you the other day?"

Now, his gaze falls away from mine, and his big chest swells. "I'm so sorry for what I did. For the way we hurt you. I know I'll never be able to make it up to you. But if you give me a chance, I want to try."

I gape at him. "I thought you hated me. That's why you ran away from Sinner's the other day."

"Hated you? What for?"

"I stopped you and your buddies from going to college."

He gives a snort. "*We* stopped ourselves. *We* were the bullies." He closes his eyes for a beat. When he opens them again, they're full of pain. "I'm not letting myself off the hook, Elinor, you have to believe this. I take full responsibility for my actions. I was an asshole. An immature prick who didn't have the courage or the smarts to break away from those assholes I called my friends. But when I found out that you were all being bullied into writing our essays for us, I wanted no part of it.

"And afterward, when you blew the whole thing open, I should've stopped, it but I didn't. I'll never forgive myself for that."

I stare at him, my head spinning.

There's a crash of drums from the stage behind us, and the lead singer struts on, screaming to the audience.

"Come on." Blake straightens up again, reaches for my hand.

"Huh?"

"Let's get you cleaned up."

I'm so stunned, so knocked off balance by what I've just heard, that all I can do is slide my hand into his huge one, and...

Follow him?

He leads me across the dancefloor, using his free arm to make sure no one else smashes into me. Guys scatter as he faces them down with his bulk. Female eyes turn in his direction. I'm not surprised. He's the hottest guy here by miles.

He brings me to the female washroom, and with no hesitation, walks right in.

There are two girls in there, doing their eyeliner in the mirror.

I watch their reflections as they do a double take,

exchange a glance, then a pair of hungry smiles spread across their faces.

"Good evening, ladies," Blake says. "I'm real sorry to barge in like this, but could we please have a moment to ourselves?"

Another glance is exchanged as curiosity and intrigue gives way to disappointment.

"Let me buy you a drink for the inconvenience." He pulls a wad of cash from his back pocket, peels off two twenties and holds them out.

The girls look from him, to each other and back again. Then, in perfect harmony, they snatch up the bills, grab their purses and dash out of the room.

"Smooth," I say, like I'm not secretly impressed.

Blake ignores my comment. "Okay, let's check you're not hurt." His hands go to my hips, but I tug away.

"I'm fine," I mutter.

"Elinor—" His voice is low, commanding.

And a dart of fire and ice runs through me from head to toe.

"Let me check."

My cheeks warm, and slowly I turn my back to him.

Is Blake Waldgrave really examining my denim-clad ass and thighs?

Apparently, he is. He crouches down, and he takes his time, while I wait, a hand clapped over my mouth to stop myself from blurting out something embarrassing. No guy has ever looked at my ass in such detail before. It's hella awkward, but mixed with another, much more pleasurable feeling.

Then he touches me, and I almost levitate.

"Hold still. I need to check there's nothing embedded." He runs his fingertips—just the nails, really—over my thighs, starting at my knees and moving, up, up.

I bite down on the knuckle of my thumb. I want him to stop.

I want him to keep touching me like that forever.

"Oh—there's one," he murmurs. I feel him plucking out a sliver of glass. All my senses are turned up to the max. I hear the tiny tinkle as he drops it on the side of the sink.

He's at the top of my thighs now, where my flesh is more sensitive.

He sweeps back and forth, every stroke bringing tingles with it.

Oh, god. I work to stay silent. To not allow a sigh or a moan to escape my lips.

Then he slides up, to my ass. If he thinks this is intimate, he gives no sign of it. Instead, he makes more little back-forth motions with his fingernails.

"One more." He plucks out another shard.

Then he lays both hands flat on my ass.

He's cupping my ass cheeks.

This can't be happening.

I hold still, suppressing a whimper, while he strokes them all over, carefully, not missing a bit. It feels like a massage.

It feels like foreplay—

An image bursts into my mind.

Me, facedown on a bed, naked, and those big hands stroking me all over, caressing me, arousing me, until I'm begging for—

I tear myself away from him.

"I'm good," I mutter. "Thanks."

But when I turn to face him, I swallow down a gasp.

There's no mistaking the hunger in his eyes.

He wants me.

I've never had that sense from a guy before, but there's no mistaking it. His werewolf eyes glow with raw hunger. I shudder, my nipples and pussy burning.

"Elinor—" he says, his voice low and throaty. He sweeps me onto the washroom counter, steps close, and—

He's kissing me.

Blake Waldgrave's mouth is touching my own.

His stupidly gorgeous lips are sliding back and forth against mine.

Oh, *wow*. And they feel amazing.

A sigh breaks out of me as I cling to him.

So soft, lush.

Passionate.

He angles his jaw, forcing my lips apart, and we're French kissing.

I have no idea what I'm doing, but I follow his lead, welcoming the intrusion of his velvety tongue, letting it slide deep into my mouth.

So good.

I feel like he's eating me alive.

Then his big hands tangle in my hair and he pushes my thighs apart, his big body sliding between them.

Forgetting my shyness, I wrap my legs around him, drawing him closer, and I feel it—

The bulge beneath his zipper, pressing right against my core.

Sweet Jesus.

Another dart of arousal shoots through me, and I *let go.* I quit thinking. Worrying.

I just go with my instincts.

I'm like a wanton beast, kissing him as hard as he's kissing me, running my hands up the back of his T-shirt, feeling his powerful, athlete's muscles.

I want him.

I want him naked.

Inside me.

I want his cock to take my virginity—

Bang!

The bathroom door bursts open and someone tries to come in. Blake draws back for a moment and kicks it shut.

"Let's go, baby bird," he growls against my lips. "I'm taking you home."

Gently, he lifts me down from the counter, kissing me all the time.

Home? To his lair?

Reality crashes back.

I've been making out with my bully.

After all I've been through.

After all the work I've done on myself, fixing my broken wings.

It's fucked up.

I tear myself away.

Can't do this to yourself, Elinor.

I grab hold of the bathroom door handle. "I've got to

go!" My voice comes out too loud and squawky.

"Yes, with me." Blake catches at my hand, but I rip it away.

"No. I've gotta get back to Perdue. I've got an early shift." I yank open the door and charge out.

My heart is hammering. I need to be alone. Need to hide my head under my wing and shut everything out.

Especially Blake Waldgrave.

I keep going all the way through the venue. I barely notice the pounding music, the screaming crowds. My fight-or-flight impulse is activated, big time. If I had real wings that worked, I'd be using them right now to jet off into the night sky.

Instead, I burst through the exit, and I run, all the way to my little car.

Blake is right there, on my shoulder. Every nerve in my body is aware of him.

He calls me, two, three times, but I ignore him.

I snatch my keys out of my purse. Fumble them. Drop them in the dirt.

His hand moves, lightning fast, snatching them up.

"Let me."

"No, I've got it."

"Elinor—"

I hate the effect his voice has on me, especially when it gets all bossy like that.

I feel a part of myself yielding to him, even as I'm grabbing the keys from his hand.

But now my hands are shaking so bad, I can't even get the key in my stupid car's ancient lock.

"I'm just trying to help you." His voice is gentle now.

A sigh rushes out of me. I go slack and let him unlock the door, and hold it open for me.

I tumble in and collapse into the seat.

He catches the door before I can slam it shut.

"I'm sorry if I freaked you out, or did something wrong tonight." His eyes are so unguarded, they tug at a place deep inside me.

"I get that you probably hate me. But I swear, I'll make everything up to you."

I shake my head, too pent up to speak.

"Come work for me. I'll pay you whatever you ask. Three times your old salary."

I shake my head. "Because you feel guilty?" I demand. "You think it'll ease your guilty conscience?"

"No. Because…" His face kind of lights as he takes me in. "You're the best."

I give one of my automatic snorts. "You don't know that."

"I've been watching you all night. And the night before that. And the night before that. I've seen how badass you are." His voice is like a caress. "I know."

"No." My voice is that awful squawk again. "You don't know me, Blake Waldgrave. You never will. Now, let me go, goddamnit."

Emotion wells up in my chest, and I tug at the door until he relinquishes his hold on it. I slam it shut, put the car in reverse, and screech backward out of the lot, before he has to see me burst into tears in front of him.

7

Blake

I'm striding down the hallway, my girlfriend, Lacey, tucked under my arm, and a bunch of my buddies flanking me on both sides. Acting like kings of the world, as usual.

Then I see her:

She's standing in front of a locker, staring at a piece of paper. We're all goofing around, and I'm not even sure what pulled my attention toward her, but I notice she looks upset. She's not crying, but her forehead is all furrowed, and her narrow shoulders are shaking.

As I get closer, I see—it's not a piece of paper, but a porno pic, torn from a magazine. A girl with black braids, and three guys with their dicks out. Someone obviously stuck it in her locker. Rage pours through me. She shouldn't have to see something like that.

I charge over, snatch it out of her hand. Ball it up and hurl it at the ground.

Her head snaps to me, lips parted.

"Hey, are you okay?" I ask.

She scans me, surprise then suspicion flashing across her face.

"Come on, Blake," Lacey whines. "I need you to give me a ride home."

"Just a second," I tell her.

"What the fuck, Blake?" Her voice is loud in my ear.

"I'll catch you up."

She curls her lip at me and stalks off.

I turn back to the girl with the braids. "Who put that in your locker?" I demand.

She plants her hands on her hips. "Why do you care?" she snaps.

I recoil. I'm not used to chicks hating on me. "I... I just do—"

"Yo, Blake! What up?" A heavy arm lands around my shoulders. "We are gonna annihilate those Eastlake pussies tomorrow!"

"Yeah, with this guy!" Another guy gets me in a headlock and scrubs my hair with his knuckles. As the team's star quarterback, this kind of thing happens to me a lot. And before I know it, I'm being borne along the hallway in a huddle of my teammates.

I'm young, dumb, and I let them pull me away from the small, skinny chick with the anxious face.

But at the last moment, I turn back.

She's still standing at her locker. She's taken her glasses off, and she's rubbing at them with a cloth.

I stop walking, I'm being pummeled in all directions by my buddies, but I fight them off and hold still.

Look up, I think.

And she does.

Without her ugly glasses, her eyes are huge and radiant. When they lock onto mine, her small, rosebud mouth opens in surprise.

She looks like an angel.

She's not the type of girl I usually go for. But I've never seen anyone as beautiful as her.

I can't breathe.

I can't move.

Mine—! my wolf growls.

My entire body jolts, like it's been electrified.

"Huh?" I mutter, but my animal has fallen silent again

"Blake! Goddamit. I swear, if you don't come right now—" Lacey is whining again.

Reluctantly I tear my eyes away, turn back to my cheerleader girlfriend. But my animal is going wild inside me. I've only been shifting for a few months, and everything feels new. I don't always understand it—

I LURCH UPRIGHT WITH A GASP.

My heart is pounding, and I'm drenched in sweat.

Some dream. It was so vivid, it felt like—

It wasn't a dream. It was a memory. Buried so deep in my subconscious that I'd never thought of it until now.

But I know that's exactly what happened that day in the hall.

I connected with her—that vulnerable, brave girl that my buddies and I had been bullying.

And my wolf put a claim on her.

But I wiped the memory from my mind, because it was so different from what I'd expected for myself. Like the dumb jock I was, I thought it was my destiny to marry some superficial girl. Even when my animal was telling me otherwise.

I leap out of bed.

I've got to get back to Elinor.

MY COCK JUTS out like a flagpole as I cross the room. It's so hard, it hurts.

I jump into the shower, turn the water on ice cold. But it's no good—my erection isn't going anywhere.

I'll be quick. I encircle my thick shaft with my hand, and start to pump. Up and down, long, fast strokes.

Kissing her in the women's washroom.

Her small, sweet mouth, suddenly so hungry.

The way she wrapped her legs around me, wanting me close.

Her small, firm tits pressing against my chest.

Fuck, she's so sexy. I've never met anyone like her before.

So spiky and edgy and unique.

She's as tough and fragile as glass.

I imagine her naked, on her knees, my cock nudging past those rosebud lips—

That's it.

I explode. Ropes of cum shoot from the end of my dick, splashing down onto the shower floor.

Soon, I'll push my cock inside her, drive her wild. Make her come apart.

And then I'll give her my mark and make her mine forever.

Soon.

* * *

THERE SHE IS.

I've been waiting outside her apartment for fifteen minutes when Elinor emerges. She's all cocooned in a big red coat and winter boots, and she's wearing a little knitted hat over her glossy black hair. She knitted it herself...

And I have absolutely no idea how I know that.

Mine, my wolf growls. At the sight of her, its ears are pricked up and it's panting. It wants to launch itself at her, of course, but I force it back, force myself to stay in the shadows.

She's walking fast, like always. This baby bird doesn't seem capable of dawdling.

And what's that—? I strain my ears as a sweet sound drifts back to me. She's singing to herself. It's a tune I've never heard before. Something unusual—as beautiful and complex as a nightingale's song. What a beautiful voice. As I listen, euphoria floods my veins.

I keep my distance until she turns a corner, then I jog to catch up. I keep following her like that, all the way downtown. I thought she was on her way to work, but then she turns off Main Street, into a small side street. Not her usual route.

I dash after her. But the alleyway is empty, like she's vanished into thin air. *Weird.* A dart of adrenaline pierces me and my heart beats faster. My beast urges me on.

Her cherry blossom scent is thick in the air, and—

She's there, at the end of the alleyway, facing me.

Relief washes over me.

A small smile tugs at the corners of her lips. She *knew* I was following her. Her cheeks are flushed from the cold, and she's absolutely breathtaking.

"—I've been thinking," she says, like we were mid-conversation.

My wolf's fur burns my skin as I step closer to her. "What?"

She tilts her head to the side and regards me with her bright black eyes. "I guess I'll come work for you."

"You will?" I try not to sound too eager, but my wolf is howling, and I'm fighting the urge to sweep her into my arms and put her in my truck right now. Drive off with her and never let her out of my sight again.

"Three times my current salary, right?"

"Whatever you want." Hell, when she's mine, I'll give her everything, everything she's ever wanted and more.

She looks thoughtful, tapping her cherry lips with gloved fingertips. "But that doesn't mean I'm going to take any shit from you."

"Of course not," I say quickly. "You'll be your own boss."

"And—"

She scans me from head to toe. "It definitely doesn't mean I'm going to fuck you, Blake Waldgrave." Her tone is as cool and sassy as ever, but a tell-tale pink flush floods her cheeks.

Oh, god.

She's thinking about me taking her virginity. She's just too adorable and sexy.

I suppress a groan of need, while my cock turns as hard as a rock.

"We'll see about that," I growl.

Her brow furrows and she folds her arms. "Never gonna happen."

"Oh, it will," I drawl, scanning her deliberately. "When you're good and ready for me."

She makes a little scoffing sound. But I can see the desire in her eyes.

This is going even better than I'd hoped.

If she wants me, she can't hate me that much. All I need is to get her back to my lair, so I can start making things up to her. Show her how sorry I am for everything I did in the past.

Then, if she can find it in her heart to forgive me, I'll show her that I'm the right one for her. That she's mine.

I take a step closer. "Don't tell me you didn't want me, last night in the bathroom."

She snorts, but her cheeks are getting even redder and I can hear the little hitch in her breath.

"I could tell how aroused you were."

She gasps and spins away from me. "I need to get to work," she snaps.

Too much. I've got to pull back before I scare her off.

"I'll pick you up later."

She turns again and frowns. "Don't you have a job to go to?"

I do. My dad caught me just as I was leaving this morning and gave me a hard time for slacking off work.

I snarled at him until he backed down.

I'm trying to make the best of this crazy business plan he's cooked up, but he's sure testing my patience.

And nothing could be as important as being with my girl. Protecting her.

"I can take time off to drive you—"

"I'll drive myself." She cuts me off. "I'm independent."

"I know you are," I say. It's one of the things I love about her.

But all I want to do is take care of her. Make up for all these years.

"Laters, Waldgrave." She starts walking. "And quit stalking me."

I grin. She's sure got my number. There's no getting past a bird shifter.

But I don't care.

All that matters is that my baby bird is coming to my lair.

And it won't be long before she's mine.

8

Elinor

I pull up in the parking lot of JC's, switch off the engine and stare at the sprawling wooden building. My stomach is in a knot, and I'm tingling all over.

I'm only doing this because I need the money.

Liar.

"Shush."

My crow has suddenly started speaking, and there's no stopping her now.

I do need the money. Carolyn has been admitted to a special shifter facility for observation—which is real good news. It means they're taking her health problems seriously. But it's not cheap. I need to earn as much as I can, and ideally, that will mean quitting my job at

Sinner's and finding someone to take my place while I work here fulltime.

If I can stand to work for Blake.

And that's a big if.

It took a lot for me to come here today.

I still don't know if I'm making a huge mistake.

How could you? the child in me whispers.

After all they put you through.

After all the distance you put between your life in Perdue and your past?

But he said he was sorry.

That he'll do anything to make it up to you.

He was young and dumb.

Easily led, like teenagers are.

Neither of us are the same people anymore.

I need to put the past behind me and act like the mature professional I am.

Caw! my crow interrupts.

Because that's not the whole truth.

I know I can be professional when I need to be.

But that's not all it is.

No. The main reason why I'm sitting here, glued to my car seat, is because my panties are wet at the thought of seeing Blake again.

At the thought he might kiss me.

Try to do more than kiss me.

Would it be so bad to lose my virgin—?

"Yes it would!" I yell into the car's interior.

Twenty-three years old, and I've never been touched. Never been kissed until last night. *You really want your first time to be with your old bully?*

Even if he is the hottest guy in the whole world?

Not. Happening.

I'm going to go work for him—so long as he treats me right—collect my paycheck, and that's all.

I grab my purse, bound out of the car and slam the door behind me.

* * *

"You came." He steps out from the shadow of the building so quick I wonder if he's been watching me while I was sitting in the car. *Probably thinking you're a freak.*

Stop.

He doesn't think you're a freak.

He said you're badass. And sexy.

"Said I would." I shrug, trying to hide the fact that my heart is pounding and I'm shaking like a leaf.

"I'm glad." He flashes a big, warm smile. The kind of smile that used to make my knees weak.

Still does, truth be told.

"Let me show you around and tell you about the business."

IT's JUST after six p.m., and JC's is mostly empty, just a few grizzled old bikers sitting around at low tables. Now I'm not so distracted, I see that the interior has been totally renovated. The bar space is cozy, while the performance area is in dark colors, industrial-style. Perfect for a music venue.

"The old clientele." Blake rolls his eyes toward the bikers. "Dad bought this place up a year ago. It was a notorious biker venue. Practically a clubhouse for the *Dirt Hogs*."

"I know," I tell him. "I did a bunch of research today, when it was quiet at Sinner's."

He nods, looking impressed. "Twenty-seven murders, a full-on riot and countless arrests to its name. And even that wasn't a deterrent to my dad."

He sighs, and I throw him a questioning glance.

"When my *business-savvy* old man saw this place advertised cheap, he thought he was getting the bargain of the decade. Didn't occur to him it might come with strings attached. Like a whole biker gang."

"You couldn't talk him out of it?"

"Nope. First I heard about it was when he was showing me the deeds. He's *spontaneous* like that." He stops walking and stares blankly at the stage. "At least, he has been ever since we lost my mom."

His mom died?

And he's still grieving, I realize with a jolt. The feeling is so raw inside him, I can almost taste it. My instinct is to throw my arms around him, hug away his pain.

"I'm sorry," I say instead.

He's silent for a long, long time. Then he begins to speak, in a voice so low I have to lean in to catch his words.

"I was a freshman at high school. My dad was supposed to collect mom from her friend's birthday party, but he forgot, because he was watching the

Superbowl. She called a taxi instead. The driver was drunk. He got into a crash and—" He breaks off, his chest rising and falling.

"Before that, we were just a regular American family. Afterward—" He throws his hands out.

"My dad's been wracked with guilt ever since. He doesn't drink, thank goodness. But he often seems like he's lost the plot. Like a big chunk of his brain died that day. My older sister dropped out of college. She's been in rehab three times already. While I—I turned into a dick." He's staring at the floor, hands shoved into his pockets.

"All that time… when my buddies and I were 'kings' of the school. While I was being Mr Popular, none of my so-called friends knew my mom had died. I couldn't bring myself to tell them. I suspected they wouldn't give a shit, and I think that scared me more than anything. While my dad was having a breakdown and my sister wasn't around, those guys became my fucked-up family. But it was all so superficial. All such bullshit. I wish I could take it all back—"

He breaks off, and the eyes that meet mine at last are stunned. Shellshocked.

"I'm sorry—you're the first person from high school that I've told."

I blink several times, trying to square my old impression of him as the popular guy with the perfect life, with this picture of a lonely, grieving teen.

"I'm so sorry, Blake," I say. "That's awful. I had no idea you were suffering."

He lifts one shoulder in a shrug. "Maybe no more

than other kids. And I was lucky that I was good at football. That meant I got instant popularity. Otherwise, I would've been one of those lonely kids who never talked to anyone. The ones who got picked on." Shame flickers in his eyes.

"Didn't hurt that you were good-looking, either," I say, thinking of all those girls who used to hang off his arm.

A wry smile tugs at the corners of his lips. "You think I'm good-looking?"

I roll my eyes. "*Everyone* thinks you're good-looking, trust me. Every girl you pass gets whiplash checking you out."

His pale gaze locks onto mine, and his smile broadens. "Yours is the only opinion I'm interested in."

My heart flips.

Then I'm mad at myself for being flattered, all over again. "Am I... like some kind of conquest for you or something?" I blurt out. "You've screwed all the pretty girls. Now you want to screw the weird chick, before you settle down with the homecoming queen and make some beautiful babies together?"

Damn, my voice is getting all squawky again. Because I'm pretty sure I've hit the nail on the head and I really wish I hadn't.

"No!" His voice is so loud I jump. "You're mine, Elinor. My mate." He reaches for my hands. When our fingertips meet, it feels like electricity is crackling between us. I yank my hands away and stuff them under my armpits, like a child.

"Don't you feel it?" he growls, low and throaty.

Crap. I wish his voice didn't have that habit of vibrating right through me. My whole body feels like it's combusting right now. I feel hot and flustered and desperate to flee.

"I don't feel anything," I lie. "That thing in the bathroom… it shouldn't have happened. From now on, it's just going to be business between us."

He recoils, hurt chasing across his handsome features. He inhales, his big chest swelling. Then he lets the breath out slowly.

"I understand. I know I hurt you a lot back in high school, and I've got a lot of making up to do. But I'm not going to give up on you, Elinor. You're my mate. And when I've claimed you, I'm going to spend my life making you the happiest woman alive."

I stare at him in stunned silence, trying to get his words to fit into my poor brain.

He thinks I'm his mate.

Because his wolf has chosen me?

Which is a real weird coincidence, because my little crow is also insisting that he's my mate.

I believe in fated mates, of course. All shifters do. To the human world, it seems like something hokey. I had to spend a long time convincing my human friend, Ava, that it was normal. But to us, it's as basic as the fact that having sex leads to babies.

But Blake choosing me?

It just seems… unlikely. Why the hell would his wolf choose someone weird and awkward and squawky and elbowy like me, when it could choose a supermodel?

"Maybe you think I'm something different," I

manage to croak out. "But you'll go back to your cheer-leaders when you get sick of me."

"No." He shakes his head with great confidence. "Not gonna happen. When a wolf chooses its mate, it mates for life."

I'm trying to be cool and unflustered, but tingles are running through me, and I'm kind of entertaining the thought of being this wolf's mate. How will his friends react when they see me on his arm? I'm sure their eyes will just about fall out of their heads.

"What does your wolf like about me?" I demand.

A grin spreads across his face. "You're beautiful and cool and smart and edgy and... I had a dream about you last night."

"W-what?" I shake my head at the sudden tangent.

He frowns in that way that makes him look thoughtful and too sexy for his own good. "It was a memory, actually. But I, like, dreamed it. I was walking past you in the hall at school, and... and—" He breaks off.

A dart of unease goes through me. "And what?"

He swipes at his hair. "Forget it. It was nothing."

I fold my arms. "Now you've put this thought in my head, you're going to tell me, Blake Waldgrave."

"You were being bullied. Again. Some kids put something in your locker."

My stomach tightens. "Was it porn?"

"Yup." He can't meet my eye.

"Not a hard guess, since it was always porn."

"I never did anything like that to you, Elinor. You've got to believe me."

I go very still. "You helped me that day." I feel like the earth is tilting on its axis. He did. He *helped* me. He wasn't the one bullying me.

"I did." His voice brings me back down to earth.

"How could I forget?"

"I forgot, too. But my wolf chose you that day. Guess it seemed so out there, my brain just couldn't process it."

"*Out there* because I was a weird-looking nerd?"

"No—because I was a dick who had girls falling—" He breaks off again, works his jaw back and forth.

"You can say it, Blake. You had girls falling all over you."

"I guess," he says in a low voice. "And you were not impressed by me, at all."

I give a snort. "Because I was supposed to be?"

He sighs. "Do you have to be so darn prickly?"

"How else am I supposed to be?" I snap. My voice is even hurting my own ears. But his eyes turn… tender?

"Just yourself," he says. "Just be your beautiful, birdy self."

My heart pounds.

Just be myself?

I never in a million years thought I'd meet a guy who wanted me to just be myself. Let alone this ridiculously hot guy.

Blood rushes in my ears, and suddenly, my eyes are stinging.

I stagger, pass a hand across my forehead, but he's right there, catching me.

"Elinor? Are you okay? Come on, take a seat."

He's leading me over to a low table, pulling a chair out and helping me sit down.

"Can't be fragile," I mutter. "Gotta stay strong. Don't let them see your vulnerability."

Oh, god, what am I saying?

Now he's really going to think I'm a freak.

"Did I upset you?" He squats down, lays his hands on my knees and looks up into my eyes.

"No. No—you were kind."

He gives a sigh of relief.

"Guess I'm not used to kind. I mean, from guys."

He reaches up and swipes my hair out of my face. "I'm going to be kind to you all the time, Elinor. You'll see. I'll give you so much kind, you'll get sick of it. You'll beg me to be a dick, just for a while."

"Not gonna happen." I laugh and swipe at my sniffly nose.

And... while I'm distracted, he swoops in, and suddenly he's kissing me again. Those lush lips are crushing against mine, soft but hungry. Ohh, his mouth feels so good. I should pull away, but I don't. I just let myself fall into this bliss.

A low growl escapes his lips, and he runs his big, warm hands up my thighs.

My legs are apart, and I can feel the heat between them. I wonder if he can sense it, too. I'm aching for him. I need his touch—

A door bangs somewhere behind me.

Blake tears his mouth away from mine, leaps to his feet and straightens up. "That's Dad," he mutters. "Come on, I'll introduce you."

He helps me to my feet. My legs are still shaking as he leads me to the bar, where a tall, lean gray-haired man is emerging from the back.

"Hey, dad. This is Elinor, our new marketing whiz. Elinor, this is my dad—who is sorely in need of your talents."

The older man frowns as he looks me up and down. "Blake's told me all about you, young lady."

Blake clicks his tongue in exasperation. "That's right. All good things. Which is why you should be shaking her hand and begging her to name her price."

"Don't mind my dad," he says to me. "He's not one for social niceties."

His dad growls, but when Blake continues to fix him with a fierce look, he stretches out his hand and I shake it.

"Welcome, Elinor. Glad to have you here."

"That's more like it." Blake claps his father around the shoulders. "Elinor unfortunately witnessed that crazy stunt you pulled last week."

"Oh, that." The older wolf coughs into his fist.

"I thought it was real original," I say, trying to be diplomatic. "But I think it's important to put our focus on the quality of the venue, and the acts we're hoping to attract."

Blake flashes me a secret, grateful smile. "Elinor's going to discuss a business plan with us later, but for now, I wanted her to see a typical night in the venue."

. . .

BLAKE'S DAD stays behind the bar, while Blake continues showing me around.

"You made a really good impression on him," he says.

"I did?"

"Very." He laughs. "Trust me, that's dad being excitable."

I smile, appreciating the way Blake handles his father. I can see he's not an easy person to deal with.

Then I stop dead as something occurs to me. "You could've played football without going to college. You gave up on your dreams to help your dad, didn't you?"

His chest rises as he takes a big breath in. "Honestly, I could've still gone to college. I got the grades by myself. Without bullying the other kids—" He breaks off with a mirthless laugh. "But after what happened, I still felt like a cheat. A phony. So I didn't go. I stopped playing football. I drifted for a few years. Couldn't get my shit together. Then my dad cooked up this crazy idea, and I thought I might as well do something good for someone."

My breath rattles through my chest.

Drifted for a few years.

He didn't give up his dreams to help his dad—that came later.

He gave them up because of what he—well, mostly his buddies—had done.

He atoned for what he did.

The thought burns sharp and bright inside me.

"Come on," Blake strides off, like he wants to change the subject.

He shows me around the floor, the stage, then he

takes me out the back and runs me through the schedule.

"What do you think?" he asks me, ten minutes later. There's a hesitancy in his voice, and I shouldn't find it as appealing as I do.

"I love it," I say.

His eyebrows tug together. "Really? All those mean old bikers hanging around? You should see the fights that break out sometimes."

I shrug. "So happens that I know a bunch of ex-MC shifters in Perdue, who I'm sure would be only too happy to run them out of here." I turn around slowly, clasping my hands. "I think this place has so much potential. It's real well-located to entice bands to come from out of state. I'm going to invite Cyclopania. I did some promo for them a while back. And SilverRun. Ooh, and Dead Fox Parade told me to get in touch if I knew of any cool up-and-coming venues. I might be able to get them to do a secret gig here—"

I break off, because Blake's eyes are sparkling, like he's *impressed* by me?

"You're amazing," he says. "You know that?"

"Nope. Not at all."

He reaches for my hand, and this time, I let him take it, envelope it in his own huge one. "You are, Elinor. "You really have no idea how special you are."

I wrinkle my nose. "I'm ordinary."

"That's the last thing you are." His expression turns real serious. "I heard you singing this morning."

"Oh, god—" My cheeks warm. "Usually, I only sing in the shower."

"It was beautiful. You've got a lovely voice. If I didn't know better, I would've guessed you were a nightingale."

"Nope. I'm all crow." I laugh. "My family thought the cuckoos dumped me in their nest, but, with these eyes and this hair—? There was never really any doubt."

He's staring at my hair again, like he's fascinated by it. "Jet black," he murmurs. "You would look great on stage."

I give a kind of choked laugh. "Are you kidding?"

He frowns. "Not at all. You have these really cool, edgy looks. I can see you fronting a rock band."

"Stop."

"What?"

"That's not... not for me—" I break off, because I'm getting choked up and I don't even know why. Probably because it is my dream. A dream so big and ridiculous, I don't even want to entertain it.

Blake gives me a long look, like he's planning to argue with me, then his face relaxes. "If you say so," he says softly. "Well, you're gonna be the best promoter that ever lived."

"Yay!" I say, too enthusiastically, trying to push back on the emotions that are threatening to spill out of me. "I can't wait to get started."

"You're going to work here full-time, right?"

"I have to work at Sinner's as well—"

"No. I need you here all the time, Elinor. Can't you get someone to cover your shifts?"

"I-I don't know," I falter, taken aback by his sudden intensity. "Sinner's is my first priority."

His shoulders slump a little. "I'm sorry, of course it is. Maybe I can ask around. See if anyone's looking for bar work?"

"Okay. Great."

"Good. You can stay here, too. There's a spare room out back."

"No, it's fine, I have my own place in Perdue."

"But you'll finish real late sometimes. It's not safe for you to drive back. You'll need somewhere to crash. Let me show it to you, at least."

I open my mouth to argue, but he's already walking toward the door at the rear of the bar.

I stare at his broad back, his big shoulders, my heart pitter-pattering.

With every step I take, I'm stepping deeper and deeper into his world...

And I don't know if that's going to be good for me.

9

Blake

I wait by the door of the accommodation building, watching Elinor coming toward me. I'm going to savor every single second of this.

God knows I don't deserve her, but I'm ecstatic she's agreed to work for me.

This time is precious. An opportunity to prove to her that I've changed. That I'm not the guy I used to be. My stupid ego has gone. All I want is for her to be happy.

And one day, when she finally trusts me, I'm gonna make her my queen.

Her tight red shirt displays her perky little tits to perfection. Not wearing a bra, I think, and my boner gets even bigger. Her eyes are huge and uncertain behind her long bangs, but I sense the need in her. The scent of her arousal has been thick in my nostrils ever since I kissed her, and it's driving my beast insane.

I have to go slow with her, though. After all I've done to her, I have to make sure she's coming to me of her own free will. That she's forgiven me.

She comes to a stop in front of me, hands on her hips. All sassy again. "This is it?"

"Yup. This is the staff quarters." I show her in. "Dad's room is here, on the first story. There's the kitchen. And the spare room's up there."

It's actually my room. But I don't tell her that. She can stay there by herself, if that's what she really wants.

I let her go up the stairs ahead of me, my eyes clinging to the small, perfect curve of her ass in those tight black jeans.

Claim her, my wolf insists. I push it back. "Not yet," I growl. I have to make sure she's ready for this.

"Go ahead," I say, when she hesitates in front of the bedroom door. She turns the handle and pushes it open. I watch her take it in. I just bought a brand-new king-size bed and a bunch of soft furnishings. Kind of extravagant for this little place, but I wanted to make it perfect for her. Especially if she lets me claim her here. I want her to think of it as a special place for her first time.

Her nose wrinkles in suspicion. "This is your room, isn't it?"

I grin. Nothing gets past a crow.

"It is. But it's for you now."

"But where will you sleep?"

Right beside you.

"Uhh, I can crash with my dad or something."

"This is... real nice," she says, confusedly.

I laugh. "Were you expecting an old mattress on the floor or something?"

She turns to face me. "I mean, when you said it wasn't much—"

I want to tell her I tried to make it nice for her, but I don't want to scare her off.

She might be aroused, but I see she's still flighty. The slightest wrong move could send her running.

"All clean sheets," I tell her. This is true, I just put them on this morning. "Want to see if the mattress is comfy?"

"I guess." She goes over, sits down and bounces on it a little bit.

Jesus, the sight of her tits, bouncing beneath her shirt. I'm just about ready to blow my load. And now my crotch is right on her eye line, and she's zeroing in on it again.

The tip of her tongue runs across her lips. Nervously. But her eyes are dark pools of desire. My beast pushes up beneath my skin. Alone in a bedroom with my mate. I can barely keep it inside of me.

She could have stood up again. But she doesn't.

Something is keeping her rooted there to the spot.

My breath catches. Is she waiting for me?

"Comfy bed, huh?" I say.

"Yeah," she says uncertainly.

I take a step closer. "What is it, Elinor?"

She puts her hand to her chest. "My bird... I-I don't know... I feel like... "

She's not making a lot of sense. But I know what she

means: it's telling her I'm her mate. And that's scaring the hell out of her.

Tenderness washes over me.

I sit down beside her. "If you really knew how I felt about you, you wouldn't be scared." I reach out, sweep the bangs from her face.

She meets my gaze with burning eyes. "How do you feel?"

"That you're mine. My mate. The one I've been looking for all my life. That I want to make you happy. Cherish you."

A gasp catches in her throat.

While her lips are still parted, I dip my head and capture them with my own. They're warm, soft, and I feel her yield to me.

When I slip my tongue into her mouth, she gives a little moan.

Holy hell.

I slide my hand beneath her shirt, over her taut stomach.

She shivers at my touch. I feel it go all the way through her. "I just want to make you feel good," I mutter against her lips.

She draws away, and gives me a long look, questions dancing in her dark eyelashes.

Then she tears the red shirt right over her head.

No bra, just as I thought, and her tits are even more beautiful than I imagined. Sweet and round, with pale pink nipples, hard with desire for me. And her slender torso is covered in tattoos of crows. Crows in-flight; resting; beautiful blue-black wings spread. It's the most incredible thing I've seen, winding all around her upper body, apart from her tits, which are left completely bare.

My beast growls.

"Who did these tattoos?" I blurt out.

"There's a shop in Perdue. A guy called Forge did most of them. The good ones anyway—"

That guy who warned me off Elinor. Who I almost challenged. My vision turns to red mist. My animal can't stand the thought of another man touching her. I'll kill him. I'll go back to his tattoo shop and tear him apart.

"He's mated—"

Elinor's voice cuts through my wolf's possessive rage.

I come back down to earth, force my animal under control again.

She's looking at me with a trace of amusement, and something else—*awe?*

"He has his mate already."

"Sorry," I grunt. "Don't like the thought of anyone else marking you."

I'm not sorry. I hope she's done inking her body, because no other man will ever touch her again.

She gets up and stands in front of me, lightly running her fingers over her taut belly. "They're important to me."

I like the way she's standing like that, confidently, not trying to hide her body from me. And I get it. This was something she did to feel good about herself. Something empowering.

"They're beautiful," I say. "Come here. Let me see them close up."

I catch her up and draw her onto my lap, so she's straddling me.

She leans back, bracing her hands on my thighs, while I examine each one, commenting on the colors and uniqueness of the designs.

I can tell she's pleased. It was the right thing to do.

"And these are the most beautiful of all." I cup my hands around her beautiful breasts, and she moans into my mouth. *God*, she's sensitive. I lift her up a little and take one of those delicate pink rosebuds into my mouth.

"Oh, Blake," she moans. I lick one, then the other, and she sighs and grinds against my cock.

I can feel the heat of her little pussy through her jeans and panties. *Fuck.* I don't want to rush her, but I can feel how ready she is. I strip off my own shirt, and she runs her hands over my pecs and shoulders delightedly.

"Haven't seen this for a long, long time, Waldgrave," she says, a hint of mischief in her voice.

I startle. "You've seen me half-naked before?"

"Only all the time." She grins broadly.

"You were checking me out?"

"Yeah, I might have been. I hated your guts, but I couldn't help noticing you were damn fine." She presses her lip to mine, pushes her bare breasts against my chest. She's so soft, so velvety.

I need out of our clothes. I ease her off my lap, tear my own jeans off, then I unfasten the button on her jeans and slide down her zipper. Her panties are lace and emerald green, and sexy as hell. When I tuck my fingertips into the waistband, her hands flutter down to stop me.

I pause. "Too fast?" I ask.

"Yes... no... I'm just a little—" She releases an epic sigh. "—you know, I haven't done this before?"

Another arousal bomb hits me, and my beast roars at the reminder of her virginity.

"I know," I say. "I'm not going to do anything you don't want me to. Don't worry."

"I do want—" She breaks off, an adorable heat spreading from her cheeks to her bare chest.

"Let me take care of you," I say. I press my lips to her soft, flat stomach as I ease her panties down. The hair between her thighs is jet black, too. Soft and neatly trimmed. And her panties are totally drenched.

"Kind of wet, huh?" I comment.

"Yeah," she mutters, with a shy smile.

I shuck her jeans and panties all the way down and help her step out of them. And finally, she's standing in front of me, fully naked. This tiny, sassy goddess.

My throat tightens. After everything, she trusts me. And it's the most goddamn beautiful thing I can imagine.

I reach for her. Kiss her again and again. She's so ready for me, and I haven't even touched her yet. My cock is so hard, it's fit to burst. I can see it in my peripheral vision, jutting out between my thighs. She hasn't looked at it or touched it yet, like she's scared of it. But when I draw her closer, encouraging her to straddle me again, her small, soft hand suddenly wraps around it.

Fuck.

A groan escapes my throat. "Elinor, I'm not going to be able to hold back much longer if you keep doing that," I growl.

She jerks her hand away again. "Sorry."

"Don't be sorry. I've just got to take care of you first." I snatch up, and lay her down on the soft comforter. She keeps glancing at my cock, as if she's nervous of it, but curious, too. She's delicious. When she's ready, I'm going to give it to her until she can't take any more.

I spread her sweet thighs and take her in for the first time. My god, she's so pink and perfect. As I hold her legs apart, she squirms a little, self-consciously. "You're beautiful," I breathe. "Perfect little body." Then I dip my head and taste her for the first time. Her sweet virgin scent fills my nostrils, like honeysuckle and jasmine.

She's wet. Wetter even than I imagined. I try to plunge my tongue inside her, but she's too tight. Her cherry still intact.

"Oh!" she cries out, when I flick my tongue lightly over her little bud.

Another surge of desire floods me. I lick her sweet pussy all over, and her fingers tangle into my hair.

"Oh, Blake—" I love the way my name sounds in her mouth. The way her body jerks and twitches and her hips start lifting right off the bed.

She needs me inside her.

And I need to mate her, more than I've needed anything in my life.

She trembles and trembles. She's getting close. I

want her to come on my tongue. But I also want her to come for the first time around my cock.

"Blake… inside… now," she pants.

I lift my head.

"I need you inside me," she murmurs. Her lips and cheeks are red, and her eyes glittering.

I bound up the bed, arch over her. "Are you sure, little birdie?" I growl.

"Yes. Now. Has to happen now," she mutters, like a woman possessed. She reaches for my cock. She's such a delightful combination of inexperience and eagerness.

And that's all the encouragement I need. I press my cock to her entrance. She's so tiny. I've got to go slow. I work it back and forth, sliding in a little, letting her get used to me. Her hands and thighs twitch, drawing me closer, pushing me away again.

"So big—" Then, "Blake—inside me."

"That's what I'm doing, honey," I growl. "Gonna push my big cock inside you. Take your virginity. Make you mine."

"Yes," she pants.

I push a little more in, and she gasps.

I withdraw a little. *Jesus.* She's gripping me so tight. I'm gonna blow my load before I get inside her.

"More," she gasps.

With a grin, I slide in another inch.

She gives a wild cry. I go still. But she grabs my hips. "Give me all of you," she pants. "I want it. I want you to claim me."

I cage a roar behind my teeth, and I push my cock all the way into her. Break through her virginity. She cries out again, while her nails bite deep into my back, and her legs wrap around me, pulling me tight to her.

"Fuck!" she gasps.

I hit home. My cock buried deep in her sweet little pussy.

She looks up at me, stunned. "You're inside me."

"I am. All of me." I dip my head and kiss her, long and tender. My cock is pulsing, but I hold still, letting her get accustomed to it. Savoring this perfect moment.

She's mine now.

Little by little, I start to move inside her. She's so tight, but so wet, and my cock glides in and out.

"Fuck," she moans, over and over.

She clings to me as I pump faster and faster into her sweet body. "Oh, I'm going to—" she mutters.

Then it happens. I feel her pussy clench around me, then she cries out rapturously.

She's coming around my cock, and it's the most beautiful thing in the world. I can't hold on any longer. I go faster, faster, faster, and then I explode, too. My beast roars, and I shoot my seed deep inside her virgin pussy. Hot, fertile spurts. Flooding her womb.

I turn onto my side before I crush her tiny body, and snuggle her into my arms.

When she nuzzles her face beneath my chin with a sweet little sigh, gratitude floods me. After all I did to her, she let me take her virginity. And I know I hurt her —she's so small and tight. But she doesn't hate me.

I caress her soft body with my fingertips, marveling at the softness of her skin, at the intricate designs scattered all over it.

I still don't like the fact that another man marked her. But soon I'll give her my claiming mark, and that's all that will matter.

"Did you like it?" I ask.

"It was… great," she breathes. "Thank you for making it so good for me."

I laugh. "You don't need to thank me."

"Well." She shifts on the mattress, then she slides a hand down between her legs. She raises her fingers, examining them with a frown. They're slick with my seed. "You came inside me," she murmurs.

"Don't worry, you're not on heat," I tell her.

She smiles. "I think you're right. And I like that you know."

"I'm a wolf." I shrug. I slide my hand lower, to her soft inner thigh. "Of course, I know. But one day, we'll make some beautiful babies together."

She goes still. "What?"

"When I've claimed you. And you're ready, of course." I trail my fingers over her taut stomach. "I can't wait to see your belly swell with my pups."

"Blake—" She jerks away from me.

Alarm darts through me. "What? What did I say?"

"We can't have babies. We're a wolf and a bird. That's the craziest combination I can think of."

"But it's meant to be. We just mated."

"I know. I know. I wanted to. But that doesn't mean I'm your *mate*." She flips over and the look she gives me pierces me.

Ice pours through my soul.

She does still hate me. Her bird wants me. Her body

wants me, but I see in her eyes that she trusts me about as far as she can throw me.

"I'm so different from you. You're an Alpha wolf and I'm not even a real shifter."

"What do you mean?" I reach for her, but she slides even farther away from me.

"I'm a broken bird. I can't even shift properly."

The sadness on her face breaks my heart. "What do you mean?"

Her voice is low, almost a whisper. "When I was a baby, and they found me in a cardboard box, my arm was broken. My real family must've hurt me. Who knows what they did to me. But I've never been able to shift properly, let alone fly. I just turn into this ugly jumble of feathers and twisted wings."

"Oh—Baby bird." I wrap my arms around her and pull her against my body. She resists me, all sharp elbows and knees, but I'm not going to let her go. I hold her tight, caging her in the warmth of my body, while she pummels and fights me.

Slowly, slowly, she stops struggling, and a pained, strangled sound escapes her lips.

I rub her back gently. "You can trust me, Elinor," I tell her.

When I stroke her cheek, I discover it's wet with tears.

"But can I?" she whispers.

I stiffen.

Of course, she can. But I can't blame her for not trusting me. Will she ever be able to trust me after what I did to her?

She sniffs loudly. "I've got to go." She wriggles out from under my arm.

"Stay here tonight. I'll get some food brought up. You can just relax. I'll bring my laptop up and you can watch movies—"

"I need to get back to Perdue." She reaches for her clothes, which are still scattered on the ground, and in a flash, she's dressed again.

I WALK her downstairs and out to her car. But she's so spiky, so turned away from me that I don't dare to press a kiss on her lips before she slides into the seat.

She slams the door and reverses out of the space without a second glance.

As I watch her drive off into the dark night, my heart aches.

My poor girl has suffered so much. She deserves the best mate, and maybe that's not me.

When she was growing up, I was part of the problem. I continued the pain her family had caused her.

How can I also be a part of the solution?

10

Elinor

*I*t hasn't gotten dark yet, and I'm driving back to JC's. Someone called Sinner's this morning, asking about the bartending job. A friend of Blake's. He's got an awesome resumé, and he came right over and did a test shift. Meredith likes him. Well, likes him well enough, anyway. She doesn't trust people quickly.

Then she chased me out of the bar and told me to go get my career started.

So now I'm heading back to Blake, to work for him full time.

My body is at war. Excitement is pricking in my chest, while my stomach is a knot of nerves. I'm scared I'm doing something bad to myself.

Ever since I've been an adult, and I've worked on my mental health, I always question whether a certain action is going to make me happier, or damage me. And right now, I can't for the life of me figure out which it is.

I mean, if I want to help Carolyn out, I don't have any choice. Blake is offering me good money. Real good money. And working in music management is what I want to do for a living. I've loved my job at Sinner's, but mainly because I love working for Meredith. My real passions have been elsewhere. But being around Blake all the time—

Well, it's a lot. Yesterday, I wanted him to take my virginity so bad. I was so ready for it. And I don't regret it one bit. It was better than I even imagined. I knew sex with him would be super-hot. But I didn't realize he'd also be so considerate, so focused on my pleasure. And now—

Now, my crow won't quit telling me I need his mark.

But I can't. I can't go down that road. It's too dangerous. I don't know if I'll ever be able to trust him. I'm scared that being with him will keep me locked in my past—after everything I've done to escape it. What if, the more I open myself to him, the more danger I'm putting myself in? What if he's only playing me, making me his conquest?

I've got a good life now. I've even made peace with the fact I might never find my mate. Not every shifter does. Am I willing to destroy everything I've built for the chance of happiness with my old bully?

It's not that I can't forgive him. I've done that already. He suffered, too. I see he's not the same man anymore. I'm just scared that my soul will wither if I don't keep my past firmly in the past.

When I pull up in the parking lot, he's already there. Standing in the doorway of the venue. And before I can even climb out of the car, he's yanking the door open.

"You came back." He surprises me with a hug.

My head is so full of conflicted thoughts, I back away from him. Confusion and hurt flash in his features, but they're gone fast.

"Meredith has hired the guy you recommended," I tell him. "So, I'm gonna be working here full time."

"That's great," he says, and he looks at me like he's drinking me in.

At the sight of him, my nipples are tingling, and so is that little spot between my thighs. Luckily, I'm wearing a bra today, but there's not a whole lot I can do about wet panties. Or the fact that my pussy is still a little sore from his cock taking my virginity.

"Today, I thought we could look at the next month's calendar and discuss which bands we can get to play?" he says.

Relief rushes through me. He's being business-like. Good. That's all I can deal with right now.

INSIDE, we sit down at one of the bar tables. Blake suggested going to the office, but I've always liked to be in the midst of things. Seems weird to plan music in a dull office environment.

Adrenaline is fizzing in my veins, and I remember that this is what I totally love to do.

The hours fly by. Blake tells me to order whatever I want from the kitchen when I'm hungry, and we have beef enchiladas. They're real good. I eat fast, as always, and I really like the way he doesn't comment on my appetite. Human guys are always surprised at how much I eat. It takes a lot of calories to keep a hectic birdie like me going all day.

It's fun working with Blake. We seem to have a lot of the same opinions on things, and he listens attentively to all my suggestions.

Meanwhile, I'm doing my best not to notice how sexy he looks in an old blue band T-shirt. It's got a bunch of rips in it, and he's apologized for it already. Said it's probably time to throw it out, but it's his favorite. But I'm not complaining, because the rips reveal swatches of his velvety, tanned skin.

I like the way he looks when he's concentrating on something, all serious and intense. Hands shoved into his hair, shuffling papers around impatiently. We're a good team, I think, and I catch myself. Because my silly bird brain was already spilling ahead, imagining us living together. Making joint decisions about how to feather our nest.

FINALLY, at nine p.m.,. Blake calls time on our session.

"But there's so much more to do," I protest.

"We did a lot of work today," he says. "We've got to pace ourselves. This is just the beginning." He leans back in the chair and stretches, and my eyes zero in on his huge pics rippling beneath his thin T-shirt.

He straightens up again and I see him noticing my attentions. "I couldn't stop thinking about you all day."

His voice is rough, growly, and just like that, the bomb detonates.

In a flash, he's gone from employer, to the guy who mated me yesterday and took my virginity. I can't breathe.

"Tell me you feel the same," he says when I don't answer.

"I was too busy to think about sex," I manage to say.

A grin spreads across his face. "Liar. I've been picking up your scent all night long. I know exactly what you're thinking about right now."

"You have no idea, Blake Waldgrave," I snap.

"Fine, I'll tell you what *I'm* thinking about." He jerks forward in his seat, leans across the table.

"I'm thinking about peeling all those little clothes off. One by one, until you're all bared to me. Then driving you crazy with my mouth. Licking your little pussy until you're begging me to take you again."

Desire rolls through me, and my pussy begins to ache.

"Not at all. You're dead wrong."

He crooks an eyebrow. "Fine then. You're thinking about my big, thick cock entering you again. How it's gonna feel sliding in and out of you." A little growl escapes his throat and his pale irises are glowing. "I want to take you in every single position, little birdie. I want to take you so hard and deep, you can't think about anything else."

I lean closer, too, until our lips are only inches apart. "And what if I told you that last night was a one-off? Maybe I just decided it was time to lose my virginity with a sexy guy? And now I want to keep things purely business?"

His nostrils flare. "I'll respect that. I won't pretend I wouldn't spend every spare minute jerking off and thinking about you, Elinor. But I can wait for you. You're my mate and I'll wait the rest of my life if I have to. My wolf has chosen you, and that means there'll be no other."

My mouth falls open. "You really mean that?"

"You're mine, Elinor."

I close my eyes. *Mine*, my bird is repeating inside me. *Mate.*

"I'm going to stay tonight," I tell him. "But that doesn't mean anything."

He gives a deep nod. "I understand," he says, but his words are belied by the glitter in his eyes.

"I'll just go get my overnight bag from the car." I leap to my feet and dash outside, desperate to break the tension between us.

It's cold. It must've dropped fifteen degrees since I arrived, and the frigid air is like a slap in the face. But it does nothing to dampen my arousal. All these years I've lived without desire. My body dormant, while all my friends find their mates, and talk about their sex lives, and how great it all is. And here I am, with Blake Wald-grave acting like he can't get enough of me.

Would it be so bad to have sex with him until I figure out what I want?

I grab my bag from the trunk of my car.

Yes, it would. Because it changes everything—and I know it.

* * *

THAT RESOLUTION LASTS AS LONG as it takes me to walk up the stairs and dump my bag on the bed.

"Elinor," Blake says softly from behind me. I turn, and he's right there. His huge, muscular presence filling my field of vision. I zero in on the bulge of his cock as it strains against his zipper, while his eyes rake over me from head to foot. My whole body is on fire with want for him.

"Want me to leave you?" he asks.

I shake my head.

In another second, I'm up in his arms, my legs wrapped around his waist while he presses me against the bedroom door, kissing me roughly. "I'm going to fuck you again," he growls in my ear. "You want that?"

"Uh huh," I manage to say.

"Tell me," he insists. His cock is rubbing against my pussy. Driving me crazy.

"I want you inside me, so bad."

He gives a growl of satisfaction and lets me slide down to the ground.

WE TEAR at each other's clothes before we fall, half-naked, onto the bed. He strips off my panties and spreads me again, examining my most private parts. "Beautiful," he murmurs. "Are you sore from yesterday, little one?"

"A little," I admit.

He strokes me gently with his fingers, chafing my

clit, making me squirm with embarrassment and pleasure mixed together.

When he slides a finger inside me, I gasp. So much
smaller than his cock, but I'm as sensitive as hell. He
slides it in and out, curling into me, seeking out the
most sensitive spots on my insides. He adds a second
finger and starts to pump, watching the whole time, as
his fingers slide in and out of me.

Fuck, this feels good. "I want—" I gasp out. At the
same time, I reach for him. His zipper is close. I
unfasten it and his cock springs out. When I wrap my
hand around it, he hisses between his teeth. Gently,
experimentally, I run my hand up and down it. I've
never seen a cock up close before, and I'm fascinated by
the size and weight of it. By the precum leaking out of
the head.

"Want to taste you," I murmur.

"Elinor—" It sounds like a warning, but before he
has time to stop me, I shuffle across the bed and lick the
tip of his cock. It's salty, sweet, and I know right away, I
want it deep in my mouth. I open wider, and start to
take him in. He gives a groan of pure pleasure, which
vibrates all the way through me.

"Elinor," he mutters my name again and again, while
I slide my lips up and down his shaft. He's not easy to
take, but I want to make him feel good, like he's making
me feel. He starts to move his hips a little bit, back and
forth. He's thrusting into my mouth. I love the
sensation.

Then he scoots along the bed, and he's licking me,
too. *Wow.*

The two of us, pleasuring each other with our mouths. And he's so good with his tongue, circling it around my aching clit. Already I'm starting to tremble. It builds, faster and faster, and suddenly, I explode, right in his mouth. His cock between my lips.

I wonder if he's going to come in my mouth, too. But he pulls out, turns me onto my back, and gently penetrates my wet, throbbing pussy.

He goes slow at first, but when I start to cling to him, crying out for him to go deeper, I feel him let go. And I come. All over his cock. Again and again, while he plows into me.

"Mine," his beast growls in my ear, over and over. I don't even know if he's aware of it, but with every thrust, I feel like I'm his.

How on earth am I going to keep my heart safe when he fucks me like this?

11

Blake

*W*hat to do when you've fallen for a little bird, whose nature is to fly away, because of what you did?

IF YOU LOVE SOMEONE, *set them free.*

And if they're yours, they'll come back to you.

And if they don't, it's because you screwed everything up when you were a fucked-up young idiot...

FOR THE PAST FEW WEEKS, Elinor has barely left JC's. We work all day and all evening. And all night long, we mate.

We're insatiable. As hungry for each other as the

first time. I can't get enough of my little crow. Her jet black hair. The startling contrast between the feathers etched all over her skin and her pale tits, with those tender nipples. That tiny pussy that stretches around my cock. I can't believe how she can take all of me, in every position. I love to hold her up while I'm fucking her. She feels weightless, like a bird in flight. Her beautiful face glowing with ecstasy. I love the way she takes me in her mouth, touching herself while she does, as if the feeling of me between her lips is driving her crazy. I've never met a woman like her before.

And she's mine.

But I don't know if she'll ever *really* be mine.

What a goddamn paradox.

Will she fly away one day and leave my soul in tatters?

I'd search for her to the ends of the earth. But I know a bird can fly to places that a wolf can't reach.

As long as I've made her happy in the meantime, I tell myself. That's what counts.

Elinor is a big success at her job—just like I knew she would be. Bands start coming to play at the venue. Good bands. And she's a genius at bringing the crowds. Every night, the place is full to bursting, and the bar sales are awesome. And at long last, the impossible happens—JC's starts to turn a profit.

My dad is ecstatic.

"Not such a dumb idea after all, was it, son?" he keeps saying. I grit my teeth. Try to distract myself by catching a glimpse of Elinor, wherever she is—usually rushing around, talking to ten people at once. She's blossomed these past weeks. That edgy watchfulness has gone, replaced by a new self-confidence. I see her starting to think of herself as the sexy woman that I see when I look at her.

I'm in love with her, but I don't know if she feels the same way about me. She's sweet and affectionate. But I feel her holding her heart away from me. And I know I can't push her. I don't have the right. My beast needs to be humble and reined in and wait for her, as long as it might take.

So, even though I wake up early every morning, just so I can watch her sleep for a while, the words, *I love you* burning on my tongue, I don't say them to her. I don't force something that she's not ready for. Instead, I try to watch the signs. I tell myself that she's always with me. That she sleeps in my bed every single night.

But the more rational part of me knows that it's practical for her to stay. The proximity I forced so I'd have time to win her heart also prevents me from knowing whether she'd choose to stay with me if we didn't work together. And that knowledge eats away at me. Maybe I'll have to be content with being her admirer. With protecting her, cherishing her, and making her come like crazy—

Impregnate her, my wolf growls. *Fill her with your seed.*

And it's so goddamn tempting. If she had my baby pup growing in her belly, she could never leave me. She'd be bound to me forever.

But I'm not that selfish anymore.

Because I know she's not ready to have a child. She's just at the beginning of her career. She has a bright future ahead of her, and there's plenty of time for her to have pups later. So, when she comes into heat in a few days, I'll warn her. And we'll have to find ways of mating that don't involve filling her sweet pussy with my cum.

"YOU'RE AMAZING. YOU KNOW THAT?" I tell her one night. We're standing at the back of the venue, and I'm speaking close to her ear, because the crowd is *wild*. *Hysterical.* On the stage is Dead Fox Parade, performing the secret gig Elinor mentioned weeks ago. The tickets sold out in under two hours, and there's currently a mob of people hanging around outside the venue, begging for spare tickets.

I'm so proud of my girl, I could burst.

She shrugs. "Just doing my job," she says, but I know how happy she is that she managed to make all this happen.

The gig is awesome. The band loves the venue, the acoustics, the crowd, and it really shows. They wind up doing a four-song encore, before they reach the final crashing, throbbing crescendo of the night.

Elinor has been darting back and forth while they've been playing, but from time to time, she stops by to kiss me. She's romantic like that, my girl.

When they're done, she goes out back to check on them.

I'm caught up making sure people get out of the

venue safely, so for a while, I lose track of time. I don't notice she's been gone for a long time.

But when she comes back, her eyes are bright with tension.

My heart plummets to my boots. Because I know in that instant that the words she's about to say will change everything for us.

"What is it?" Ignoring everything else that's going on, I pull her aside.

"What happened? Did someone upset you?" My heart crashes against my rib cage, and my beast is already burning my skin, ready to destroy anyone and anything.

She bites her lower lip. "It's nothing. Forget it."

"Elinor. I want to know everything about you. Don't hide anything from me, please."

She exhales slowly. "The guys are going on tour for three months, and they've asked me to manage them. Their manager doesn't want to travel because she's pregnant, so they want me to fill in." The words come out in a rush, and I can tell she's uncertain, but excited.

"Manage them remotely, you mean?"

"Nope. On location."

I feel like I've been sucker punched.

"And what did you tell them?"

"I said I have a job already."

"You should go." I force the words out before they choke me.

"What?" She frowns.

"Elinor, it's a great opportunity. This is what you've always wanted, right?"

"I guess."

"So?"

"Well, I thought you'd freak out when I told you."

"I want you to follow your dreams."

"I am. I mean, I'm managing this place."

"But they're an international band. This is bigger than JC's—" I break off because my beast is whining in confusion.

I want to tell her not to go. Of course, I do. I can't stand the thought of her not being with me. Of her being around other men. But I don't have the right.

After all the things I did to limit her happiness in the past, I've got to let her free.

I know it deep inside.

And the knowledge tears me apart.

"The calendar is almost full for the next three months, anyway," she says.

"Totally. And I can take over, now I know how to do stuff."

"You won't even need me."

"Yeah. We'll be fine," I say, and the words come out way harsher than I intended. Hurt chases across her features.

I could take it all back now. Tell her I didn't mean it. My beast is howling in pain. Howling for me to make the right decision.

To beg her not to leave.

To stay with me forever.

But I don't.

"When do they want you to start?" I ask instead.

"They're playing in LA in two days," she says. "So, then."

My beast roars. I step away from her before I lose control of it.

"Go, and be happy," I say.

I GAVE HER WINGS.

And they helped her fly the nest.

It was the right thing to do.

To atone for all the damage I did her.

But I can't pretend it doesn't hurt like hell.

12

Elinor

*I*t's better this way. This way I don't have to watch Blake get tired of me. Leave me broken and in tatters. These past few weeks, it's taken me every last bit of my willpower not to fall hopelessly in love with him.

And I've failed—mostly. I've given him almost all of my heart.

There's just that little bit that tells me, *don't trust him—*

This is not my bird speaking, by the way. My bird is all in.

Mate,

Mine,

is blasting in my ear all day long.

It's the sensible, cautious part of me. Which believes he's trying to get rid of me.

Blake is sweet and attentive, and he acts like he loves me, but he's never said the words, so I guess he doesn't mean them. He's not the kind of guy to hold back.

He's not the guy I thought he was. At all. He's everything I could want and more. So strong and protective, but he doesn't take away my independence.

He lets me be me. It's like he understands my flighty bird heart.

But maybe he's losing interest now he knows me better. He didn't sound so crushed that I was leaving.

I'M LOOKING out the window of an airplane, watching the ground get smaller and smaller. Perdue is down there, and so is Arndale, but I can't see them. And so is Blake.

The band collected me, in their private jet. It's like a dream. And before I'd met Blake, it would've been my dream. But now, leaving him hurts so bad, it's all I can think about.

I've got to pull myself together. Enjoy this experience. There's nothing keeping me back in Perdue. Carolyn is on the mend, thank goodness. It turns out the problem was with her inner ear, and it's treatable. We are all so, so relieved.

Before I left, Blake gave me a pep talk. Told me to make the most of every minute—to enjoy my dream to the max. He'll be waiting for me when I get back.

I know that's not true. Three months is a long time. He will have met someone else. Of course, he will. Girls *salivate* over him in JC's. Whenever we're together, there are a ton of eyes watching him with lust, and me with bitter envy. I've tried to be cool with it, but some days, when I'm not feeling my best, those voices start up again.

They're wondering what a hot guy like him is doing with a weird-looking chick like you.

Blake and I are just too different. I'll always cherish our time together, but we don't belong together. He'll end up with an ex-cheerleader, and that's how things are supposed to be. And I... well, I've gained a ton of confidence since I've been with him. Maybe I'll be able to go out into the world and find—

Mate!

Wow! That squawk is deafening. I resist the urge to clap my hands over my ears. Not that it would do any good, since my bird's voice is in my head.

No, I'll probably live the rest of my life alone. Since my bird has already chosen Blake, the stubborn little thing is unlikely to accept another.

"Hey, Elinor!" I jerk away from the window, discover I've been drawing a heart in the condensation.

I look for the lead singer, Rick.

"Come join us over here!" he calls from behind me. "We're playing blackjack."

I stand up with a grin and go join the guys. They're great. Nothing like Umbilicus. They're all married or have long-term partners, who are here with them on the tour. No egos. No groupies. They already promised me that, without me even asking.

This is the opportunity of a lifetime, and I've got to live it. Got to justify walking away from Blake.

Even if it tears my heart apart in the process.

13

Three months later

Elinor

ears are streaming down my face. Half the band are crying, too.

It's the last night of the tour, and we're in New York. Ninety days and thirty-eight gigs later—including three secret gigs I set up—and we're done. What a ride. It's been unreal. Electrifying. So much emotion and excitement. And this final gig has just been awesome. The crowd was so loud and excitable.

I've had the best time. So many adventures, so many photos, so many great memories.

Today is my last day with the band, though. They've

asked me to work for them permanently, but I've realized two things.

One: I don't want to spend my whole life on tour. It's been a blast, but it unsettles my bird too much. I need my permanent roost. My family. I miss the guys in Perdue like crazy.

And two: I haven't gotten over Blake one bit. Not one iota. Every second that my mind hasn't been occupied by work, it's flown back to him. Painful, aching, longing thoughts. So many memories of us kissing, holding hands. Mating. Just lying in bed together, talking about our dreams.

I haven't been in touch with him. I stopped myself from stalking him on social media. Haven't even looked up JC's to see how it's doing. Because I know he will have moved on. And, that's right.

He hasn't called or come looking for me, either. Ninety percent of me is glad for that. But the other silly little part wished he'd checked on me... and hurts like hell for the fact he let me go so easily.

I've got to get over him now. I'm stronger than I was three months ago. I've got to take my heart back to Perdue and build my life there. The band has given me a real generous bonus, and I'm thinking, maybe I can start up my own little live music venue in Perdue. There's a ton of empty shops there, crying out to be converted—

"Elinor, come celebrate with us!" Jennifer, the lead singer's wife yells, shoving a JD and coke into my hand. I say cheers with the band and pretend to sip it. But the truth is, I haven't been able to touch JD since I walked out of Blake's life. Just the smell of it takes me back to that night when he picked me up off the floor, cleaned all the broken glass off my ass, then kissed me senseless.

I thought Blake belonged to my past, but I was wrong. He's a part of who I am now—he gave me wings to become who I really am.

But I still need to put him behind me.

The after-show party gets louder and louder, then Jennifer pulls out her karaoke machine, and everyone groans.

She loves singing as much as her famous husband does, but unfortunately, she's tone deaf. A fact she's aware of, but after a few drinks, nothing's going to stop her. So, she cranks up the machine and starts belting out her favorite songs. The more people complain and jam their fingers in their ears, the louder she gets.

"Girls, come join her," Rick says, beckoning to us desperately. "See if you can drown her out a little," he mouths when she's not looking.

"Come on, Elinor!" Kimberley, one of the other wives, grabs my hand and drags me over to the machine. One ear-splitting song finishes, and everyone squabbles over what to sing next.

"Oh—I got it!" Jennifer jabs at the screen triumphantly. "I used to love this one when I was a kid." She hits play.

And shivers race down my spine. Because it's my song.

The one that used to give me comfort and courage when I was a lonely teen. The one Blake was singing that first night at JC's.

"Okay, one—two—three—four—" Kimberley counts

us in. I close my eyes, take a deep breath and start to sing.

I sing the intro, the first verse, and the chorus…

And I realize that no one else is singing.

My eyes fly open. The girls have fallen silent, and the band is staring at me. Like they're shocked or something. I break off, confused and embarrassed.

"Keep going, girl," Rick calls, pressing a hand to his chest. "That's freaking beautiful."

My heart gives a little jump and I keep singing. These words that touched me so deeply when I was struggling so much. This tiny flicker of hope for a better future that I carried deep inside me. When I sing the last few words, my voice chokes up and I can barely finish.

There's a big round of applause from the room.

"Geez, Elinor, where the hell have you been hiding that talent?" Rick says.

I blink, too stunned to say anything. Out of all the rock bands I like, Rick has the best voice, in my opinion. And he thinks I'm a good singer?

And I do a double take.

Because, standing off to the side of Rick is Blake.

Huger and sexier than ever. His eyes burning with admiration and—love?

And then he's walking toward me.

"How did you… you're here!" I blurt out, making no sense at all, because my heart is pounding so hard I feel dizzy.

"I've always been here, baby," he murmurs close to my ear, as he sweeps me up in his big arms.

"You have?" I draw back and look at him confusedly.

"Nearly all the time. I had to go back and work with dad from time to time. But most nights I've been here, keeping watch over you."

"B-but you never contacted me?"

He shrugs. "You needed to spread your wings and become the person you're supposed to be. But I also knew I wasn't going to let you out of my sight. You're mine, Elinor. And I'm never letting you go."

I cling to him again, pressing my face against his big chest, my emotions spilling over. "I thought I'd never see you again."

"Are you kidding me?" he growls. "A wolf does not abandon its mate."

Mate, my bird echoes. Overjoyed that he's back.

Blake's hands run over my body, possessively, urgently. "Do you think we can get out of here soon?"

I look around, thrills racing through me.. Everyone's drinking, having fun. Jennifer is flicking through her karaoke catalogue for more inspiration. "Let's go," I say. "Right now."

* * *

HE TAKES me back to his hotel room. The place the band booked for me is nice. But this is on a different level. Five-star luxury. It's the fanciest hotel I've seen in my life. "This is unreal," I murmur as we walk through the huge glittering lobby.

"Only the best for you," Blake says, snuggling me tight against his body.

. . .

THE ROOM IS BEAUTIFUL. There's a huge, king-size bed, luxurious white furnishings, and a soft fluffy rug on the floor. There's also a ton of mirrors and a gigantic floor-to-ceiling window. Keeping his arm around me, Blake leads me over to it.

We are twenty-four stories up, and the view is awesome.

"Wow," I breathe. "You can see the whole city."

Skyscrapers, bright lights. So much energy. Blake points out all the famous buildings, as he stands behind me, nuzzling my neck.

I sigh as his lips trace a line from my neck to my shoulder. "I still can't believe you're here," I say.

"I'm never leaving you alone again." I hear him breathe in and out, hesitating. "I love you, Elinor. You know that?"

"Oh—" I turn to face him. My eyes are suddenly stinging. "I love you too, so much."

"You do?" he rushes out, like he can't quite believe it. He dips his head and takes possession of my mouth again. Long, slow, then hungry.

At last, he draws back. "I'm going to claim you now," he growls.

A shiver of excitement goes through me. "I was kind of hoping so."

He turns me around again, so I'm facing the window. Then he sweeps my hair away from my neck and kisses it again.

Instinctively, I brace my hands against the cold glass. He lifts my black silky shirt up and pulls it right over my head. Then his fingertips run all over my upper body.

Light, maddening.

He cups my tits through my bra. But when his hands go to the clasp at the back, I stiffen.

"Aren't people going to, like, see me?"

He chuckles. "Only if they've got a real strong pair of binoculars. And let them look. You're beautiful."

I swallow nervously. But the moment my bra falls off and his hands slide up to replace it, I feel sexy.

Yes. I, Elinor Earwood, weird-looking chick, feel sexy standing half-naked in the window of a skyscraper, with Blake Waldgrave running his big hands all over my body.

"You like that?" His breath is hot in my ear, while his fingers play lightly with my nipples, turning them into aching peaks.

"Yes," I manage to say.

He yanks his own shirt off, and that velvety skin of his presses up against my back.

Then his hand slides down the front of my tight black pants.

Part of me wants to stop him. The other part is desperate for him to touch me there. That little spot between my thighs that's aching for him.

When he slides his hand into my panties. I give a little cry.

"Already wet for me, huh?" he mutters, his voice thick with need. "You're so sexy, Elinor." He works a finger inside me, spreading my wetness all over.

Do I want people to see this happen?

No.

Yes.

It's overwhelming.

Jesus, I'm already clenching around him. And it's driving me crazy that I can't touch him in this position.

"Let's go to the bed," I say.

He leads me over, we strip each other's clothes off, and there he is again.

His magnificent naked body arching over me. His cock hard as a rock. Ready for me. Off to the right, the reflection of us in the mirror catches my eye. Usually, I avoid mirrors. But I'm so keyed up, so distracted by my arousal, that I turn my head and look.

And I'm shocked. Blake looks as sexy as ever. Poised over me. His big body musclebound, powerful. And I look—well—I look like a sexy woman. Passionately entwined with her man.

The thought hits me like a truck.

Blake follows my line of vision, then he turns back to me with a grin.

"Maybe we should turn the lights out," I mutter.

He shakes his head. "No way. See how beautiful you are."

I frown, and the girl in the mirror frowns back at me. "This is me?"

"Of course." He gives an indulgent laugh.

"Did you put a spell on me or something?"

"This is how you've always looked, Elinor. I've told you a million times how beautiful and sexy you are. And I'll tell you a million times more, until you believe me."

He dips his head and kisses my throat. Then the

valley between my breasts, then he takes one of my pebbled nipples into his mouth.

And I watch it all happen. For the first time in my life, I feel like I want to be seen.

I watch, entranced, as his dark head dives between my thighs and his skillful tongue slides inside me.

I only stop watching when he brings me to a climax, and all I can see is multi-colored stars.

When he lifts up again and flips me onto my front, I eagerly move into position eagerly. I'm on my hands and knees, my back arched, legs spread apart a little.

"So beautiful," he murmurs, caressing my pussy with his fingertips.

In the reflection, I see him behind me, grasping his thick shaft in his hand, jerking it up and down a few times before he presses it to my entrance.

I cry out as his cock pushes inside me, spreading me wide open. His hips butt against my ass as he hits home. All of him, buried inside me. Tingles of euphoria pour through my body.

Then he begins to fuck me, while I watch. His big muscles flexing as he thrusts into me. Me, so tiny in comparison, my ass lifted, taking all he's got to give me.

Damn, I never realized this could be so sexy.

That moment from high school flashes into my mind—when he tore that awful porno pic out of my hands.

Now I'm watching him fucking me, and it's the sexiest thing in the world.

Blake holds me tight, his thrusts getting harder and harder, while he drills me into the mattress. My legs are getting weak, and I collapse onto the bed. He lays more of his weight on me, and I feel his skin sliding against mine, slick with perspiration. His breathing is rough and growly, and his thrusts get harder, faster. I feel his lips move to the back of my neck. Gooseflesh breaks out on my skin.

Then I feel the rougher touch of his teeth, and it happens—

He climaxes with a roar, then his sharp canines bite down on the back of my neck.

"Mine!" he growls as his cum spurts inside me.

"Mine!" my bird pipes up at the same time.

BLISS POURS THROUGH ME. I lose a few minutes. Maybe I even fell asleep. When I'm conscious again, Blake's muttering words of love in my ear.

I sigh happily.

"Now we're mates. For better or for worse," I say jokily, minutes later. "You're never getting rid of me."

"For better, trust me," Blake says, snuggling me even closer. "Elinor Earwood, you're the best thing that ever happened to me."

EPILOGUE

Six months later

My heart jumps into my throat as we turn off the highway and pass onto a familiar old road.

Immediately, Blake reaches for my hand.

He knows.

He always knows when I'm stressed or worried or scared. He holds it in his big, warm grasp. Our animals connect and my pulse slows.

"You're so beautiful, Baby Bird," he murmurs.

He tells me that a lot. He tells me a bunch of other flattering stuff, too. But I think because he knows my appearance has caused me the most distress over the years, he always makes sure to compliment my looks.

"You keep telling me that and I might start to believe you," I say.

He makes a sound of mock-exasperation, and I grin.

I do believe, him, *mostly*.

Because there's no mistaking the love and desire in his eyes, so many times each day.

This morning, when I crept out of the bedroom in a long, black silky thing with a big, attention-grabbing skirt, I swear his eyes teared up. Gently, he drew me in front of the hallway mirror and stood behind me, telling me to close my eyes.

When I opened them again, he was slipping a beautiful, emerald necklace around my neck. "Wow," he breathed. "I knew it. It goes so well with your hair and eyes." My cheeks went pink as I acknowledged he might be right.

Reflexively, I lift my fingers to it. It's gorgeous. Expensive and intricate. The weight of it around my neck gives me confidence.

We pass through a bunch of smaller streets as we get closer to our destination, but the contact with Blake's hand reassures me.

We make one final turn, and suddenly—we're there.

The big, gray institutional building swings into view.

The air rushes out of me.

It's fine.

It's really fine.

I thought I might pass out or throw up or something when I came face-to-face with my old high school. But it's not the monster I've been imagining all these years. It's just a building. Smaller and shabbier than I remember.

"Are you okay, sweetheart?" Blake lays his arm around my shoulders.

"Yes. I am," I say, and I start laughing. Because it was so crazy to imagine that, with all the amazing things that fill my life now, this old place would have any effect on me. I think of all those poor, insecure kids stuffed into that building. All those egos and neuroses, and products of bad parenting. And I feel sorry for them. For every single one of them who tormented me. How much they must've hated themselves to have bullied other people.

Blake jumps out of the car and dashes around to my side. He opens the door for me. He's wearing a tux and he looks ridiculously handsome. Every time I look at him, I swoon a little bit.

"Shall we?" He offers his elbow, like a gentleman from another era, and I tuck myself against his side. I love the way we fit together—an Alpha wolf and a little quirky bird. Who would've guessed we'd be so perfect for each other?

He leads me toward the building, and my heart swells with pride.

A banner hangs over the entrance, reading *Gradwell High Class of 2013 Reunion – Welcome Back!*

There's a prickle in my stomach, but it's more anticipation than nerves.

"You're the belle of the ball," Blake murmurs, dipping his head and planting a kiss on my cheek.

"We haven't seen anyone else yet."

He shrugs happily. "Doesn't matter."

He opens the front door for me, then the second set

of doors, and we're in. Back in this weird little micro-
cosm of hormones and angst. The same scuffed old lino
flooring; the same lockers lining the same corridors.
And there's my old locker—number 349. The site where
Blake snatched the porn out of my hand, and realized
that I was his mate. It was the site of a lot of other
things, too. But I don't care about any of those. Tenderness sweeps through me. As we pass, I brush it with my
fingertips, and offer a silent blessing to whoever owns
that locker now.

At the end of the corridor is the grand hall. Music
filters through—some R&B song from back in the day.

Blake gives me one final look of pride and love, and
we sweep in.

And a million eyes turn in our direction.

They're all looking at Blake. Of course, they are.
They're all wondering what the hottest, coolest guy in
the school has been doing all these years. I smile to
myself as envy, affection and lust fills these eyes. I'm so
proud of him, I could burst.

There's a kind of pause as everyone takes him in.
And then they rush over.

What's up bro?

Where have you been?

*Thought you were dead! You haven't returned any of my
calls.*

A few months ago, I discovered that Blake hasn't
kept in touch with anyone from his high school days.
He told me he felt so bad about all the bullying and
cheating he wanted to put the whole thing behind him.
So now the curiosity is so intense, I can taste it.

Then, the crowd parts and a tall, blonde woman appears. Lacey. Blake's bitchy ex-girlfriend.

She's still striking. A head-turner. Her toned body is encased in a shimmering gold ballgown. But up close, her face looks kind of puffy, like she's had some work done on it.

"Hey, Blake," she says breathlessly. "Been a long time."

"Lacey." He gives a cursory nod.

A frown mars her smooth forehead. "That's all you've got for me? After everything?"

She throws her arms out and steps in to kiss him.

My bird ruffles its feathers and snaps its beak, ready to attack.

But Blake draws me against him more tightly. "Lacey, meet Elinor, my mate."

Lacey comes up short. Her collagen-filled upper lip draws back, and she stares at me with a mixture of confusion and dismay.

"Your mate," she repeats. As she looks me up and down, there's something else in her eyes. *Envy? No... that's not it. She looks kind of self-conscious? ... She finds me intimidating.* My heart gives a little jump of shock.

Can that be right?

Something about my appearance makes Lacey feel inadequate? I don't pretend to understand it, but I'm gonna enjoy it for the next few seconds.

This morning, Blake told me I look like *one of those supermodels. You're not the girl next-door,* he told me. *You're totally unique.* I get a warm feeling thinking about it.

"How long have you been together?" Lacey demands.

"A while, but we met at high school," Blake says, planting a kiss on my cheek.

"High school?" Lacey's mouth starts to work, and I can practically see the cogs of her brain turning. "What year?"

"Our year," Blake says.

Her eyes narrow in confusion.

"She was the smart one. She won the national spelling bee. The science prize."

"One of the nerds?" Lacey blinks, then her eyes get comically wide. "Ohh—I do remember you... Oh, my god. You were that girl who got Jeff expelled, and took down half the football team."

I feel Blake tensing beside me. But my crow communicates with his wolf:

I got this, she tells him.

"They took themselves down," I say coolly.

"And now she's your mate?" she flashes Blake a look of outrage.

"Yup. We're fated mates."

"After you dumped *me?*" She makes a kind of strangled sound.

"Speaking of Jeff, you know what I remember you for, Lacey?" I cock my head, looking at her thoughtfully.

As I hold her gaze, she stiffens, then slowly, a pink flush spreads across her cheeks and all over her chest.

Because I know she's thinking what I'm thinking... of that time I burst into the restroom and caught her blowing Jeff and one of his teammates, at the same time.

She stares at me in horror. "No," she mouths.

I hold on for another beat.

"Nothing," I say sweetly. "I don't remember you at all."

Then I turn on my heel and flounce off.

* * *

ALL NIGHT LONG, Blake keeps a protective arm around me, while we chat, snack and dance together. I'm having a lot of fun. People are interested to hear all about my work, touring with Dead Fox Parade, and about JC's which is doing real well at the moment.

Halfway through the evening, the music pauses and our old principal, Mr Montgomery, clumps onto the stage. I break into a grin at the sight of him. When I blew the whistle on the cheating and bullying, he warned me that the path I was choosing was the brave one, but not an easy one. But I shouldn't be afraid to do the right thing. And he was right. I haven't regretted my decision for a second.

He gives a speech, welcoming back the class of 2013.

"And now—" he says, beaming at the audience through his big, red moustache. "We are very lucky to have a rising star in our midst. Please put your hands together and welcome Elinor Earwood to the stage!"

"This is it, baby," Blake whispers in my ear. As the audience claps, he lays his hands on my waist and guides me toward the stage. This is my eleventh live gig, and I feel a lot less nervous than I used to, but there's still a little tightness in my stomach.

When I reach the first step, I turn and face Blake,

grasping his hands in mine. "Surprise… you're coming, too."

He frowns. "This isn't what we agreed… you were going to do a solo… "

"I need you with me Blake."

He nods. That's all I need to say. Keeping hold of my hand, he follows me up the steps and joins me center stage.

The high school band is on the stage behind us, waiting to intro the first song.

"Tonight, I was going to sing a solo for you all—" I speak into the microphone. It's still a surprise how effortlessly my voice travels across the room. "But since Blake Waldgrave is such a big part of my story, there's no way I could be up here without him. And tonight, we're going to duet a song that means a lot to us both."

I turn and nod to the leader guitarist, he plays the opening chords, and—

And the room explodes into cheering and whooping.

I had no idea how popular this song was. How many people could relate to it. We were all lonely, all hoping things would get better, I realize.

Tears prickle my eyes as I sing the intro and Blake joins me in the chorus… and suddenly, the audience is singing, too.

It's an incredible, uplifting moment. Warmth floods my entire body.

By the time I'm singing the final line, tears are pouring down my cheeks, and the applause is *deafening*.

We're all together. This bunch of totally diverse people, united in our common experiences.

"That was incredible, baby," Blake says, close to my ear.

"Because of you," I reply.

I thank my old classmates in a choked-up voice. I'm about to introduce the next song, when Blake drops down in front of me.

It takes my brain a minute to catch up, to figure out what's going on.

He's down on one knee. There's a blue velvet box, tiny in his huge hand. It's snapping open, and an emerald-green ring is sparkling. It looks very similar to the necklace around my neck, I realize distractedly.

"Elinor Earwood, I love you with all my heart and soul. I've known you're mine since that moment we locked eyes at high school—" Blake's deep voice booms around the hall. "You're the most incredible thing that's ever happened to me. And every day I wake up and can't believe you're right there beside me. We've officially been mates for six months—which is the most important thing, of course. But will you do me the honor of becoming my lawfully-wedded wife?"

I let out a gasp, and stare into his gorgeous eyes. I have his mark on my neck. Our animals are perfectly bonded, and now this… this public sign of our love.

It's so romantic, I could burst.

"Yes," I manage to say, and I fall into his embrace and kiss him, kiss him, while my bird heart soars. And all around us, whistles and cheers fill the air.

THE END

READ THE OTHER BOOKS IN THE SERIES

If you like steamy insta-love romance, featuring obsessed, growly heroes who'll do anything for their mates, check out the rest of the books in my Obsessed Mates series. All books are standalone and can be read in any order.

Continue the series at arianahawkes.com/obsessed-mates

READ MY OBSESSED MOUNTAIN MATES SERIES

If you like fated-mate romances, with plenty of V-card fun and tons of feels, check out my Obsessed Mountain Mates series. All books are standalone and can be read in any order.

Get started at arianahawkes.com/obsessed-mountain-mates

READ THE REST OF MY CATALOGUE

MateMatch Outcasts: a matchmaking agency for beasts, and the women tough enough to love them.

★★★★★ "A super **exciting, funny, thrilling, suspenseful and steamy shifter romance series**. The characters jump right off the page!"

★★★★★ "**Absolutely Freaking Fantastic**. I loved every single word of this story. It is so full of **exciting twists that will keep you guessing until the very end** of this book. I can't wait to see what might happen next in this series."

Ragtown is a small former ghost town in the mountains, populated by outcast shifters. It's a secretive place, closed-off to the outside world - until someone sets up a secret mail-order bride service that introduces women looking for their mates.

Get started at arianahawkes.com/matematch-outcasts

MY OTHER MATCHMAKING SERIES

My bestselling *Shiftr: Swipe Left For Love* series features Shiftr, the secret dating app that brings curvy girls and sexy shifters their perfect match! Fifteen books of totally bingeworthy reading — and my readers tell me that Shiftr is their favorite app ever! ;-) Get started at arianahawkes. com/shiftr

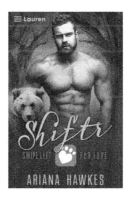

★★★★★ **"Shiftr is one of my all-time favorite series**! The stories are funny, sweet, exciting, and scorching hot! And they will **keep you glued to the pages**!"

★★★★★ **"I wish I had access to this app**! Come on, someone download it for me!"

Get started at arianahawkes.com/shiftr

CONNECT WITH ME

If you'd like to be notified about new releases, giveaways and special promotions, you can sign up to my mailing list at arianahawkes.com/mailinglist. You can also follow me on BookBub and Amazon at:

bookbub.com/authors/ariana-hawkes
amazon.com/author/arianahawkes

Thanks again for reading – and for all your support!

Yours,

Ariana

* * *

USA Today bestselling author Ariana Hawkes writes spicy romantic stories with lovable characters, plenty of suspense, and a whole lot of laughs. She told her first story at the age of four, and has been writing ever since, for both work and pleasure. She lives in Massachusetts with her husband and two huskies.

www.arianahawkes.com

GET TWO FREE BOOKS

Join my mailing list and get two free books.

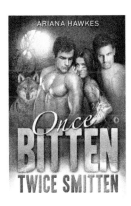 

Once Bitten Twice Smitten

A 4.5-star rated, comedy romance featuring one kickass roller derby chick, two scorching-hot Alphas, and the naughty nip that changed their lives forever.

Lost To The Bear

He can't remember who he is. Until he meets the woman he'll never forget.

Get your free books at arianahawkes.com/freebook

READING GUIDE TO ALL OF MY BOOKS

Obsessed Mates

Her River God Wolf

Her Biker Wolf

Her Alpha Neighbor Wolf

Her Bad Boy Trucker Wolf

Her Second Chance Wolf

Her Convict Wolf

Obsessed Mountain Mates

Driven Wild By The Grizzly

Snowed In With The Grizzly

Chosen By The Grizzly

Off-Limits To The Grizzly

Shifter Dating App Romances

Shiftr: Swipe Left for Love 1: Lauren

Shiftr: Swipe Left for Love 2: Dina

Shiftr: Swipe Left for Love 3: Kristin

Shiftr: Swipe Left for Love 4: Melissa

Shiftr: Swipe Left for Love 5: Andrea

Shiftr: Swipe Left for Love 6: Lori

Shiftr: Swipe Left for Love 7: Adaira

Shiftr: Swipe Left for Love 8: Timo

Shifter Holiday Romances

Bear My Holiday Hero

Ultimate Bear Christmas Magic Boxed Set Vol. 1

Ultimate Bear Christmas Magic Boxed Set Vol. 2